"Some Do Not Care About The Rules For Bride Courting,

"or the way a man and a woman choose each other," Tanner said softly. "We skipped that part the first time. We let others tear us apart."

Gwyneth shivered. "That time is gone now, Tanner."

"Is it? You kissed me hard, Gwyneth, as if you'd waited and couldn't wait a minute more. Did you think of how it would be, not only the loving, but the life we could have had, babies held close and loved between us?"

She'd dreamed of him…erotic dreams in which he'd moved over her, filled her, stroked and heated her body with his kisses. "It was only a kiss." The lie crackled around her. "Why are you here?" she asked in a shaky whisper.

"Because I have to know if we could have made it work."

Dear Reader,

This April of our 20th anniversary year, Silhouette will continue to shower you with powerful, passionate, provocative love stories!

Cait London offers an irresistible MAN OF THE MONTH, *Last Dance,* which also launches her brand-new miniseries FREEDOM VALLEY. Sparks fly when a strong woman tries to fight her feelings for the rugged man who's returned from her past. *Night Music* is another winner from BJ James's popular BLACK WATCH series. Read this touching story about two wounded souls who find redeeming love in each other's arms.

Anne Marie Winston returns to Desire with her emotionally provocative *Seduction, Cowboy Style,* about an alpha male cowboy who seeks revenge by seducing his enemy's sister. In *The Barons of Texas: Jill* by Fayrene Preston, THE BARONS OF TEXAS miniseries offers another feisty sister, and the sexy Texan who claims her.

Desire's theme promotion THE BABY BANK, in which interesting events occur on the way to the sperm bank, continues with Katherine Garbera's *Her Baby's Father.* And Barbara McCauley's scandalously sexy miniseries SECRETS! offers another tantalizing tale with *Callan's Proposition,* featuring a boss who masquerades as his secretary's fiancé.

Please join in the celebration of Silhouette's 20th anniversary by indulging in all six Desire titles—which will fulfill *your* every desire!

Enjoy!

Joan Marlow Golan

Joan Marlow Golan
Senior Editor, Silhouette Desire

Please address questions and book requests to:
Silhouette Reader Service
U.S.: 3010 Walden Ave., P.O. Box 1325, Buffalo, NY 14269
Canadian: P.O. Box 609, Fort Erie, Ont. L2A 5X3

Cait London
LAST DANCE

Published by Silhouette Books
America's Publisher of Contemporary Romance

To Kerry, a potter.

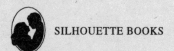 SILHOUETTE BOOKS

ISBN 0-373-76285-2

LAST DANCE

Copyright © 2000 by Lois Kleinsasser

This edition published by arrangement with Harlequin Books S.A.

® and TM are trademarks of Harlequin Books S.A., used under license.
Trademarks indicated with ® are registered in the United States Patent
and Trademark Office, the Canadian Trade Marks Office and in other
countries.

Visit Silhouette at www.eHarlequin.com

Printed in U.S.A.

Books by Cait London

CAIT LONDON

lives in the Missouri Ozarks but loves to travel the Northwest's gold rush/cattle drive trails every summer. She enjoys research trips, meeting people and going to Native American dances. Ms. London is an avid reader who loves to paint, play with computers and grow herbs (particularly scented geraniums right now). She's a national bestselling and award-winning author, and she has also written historical romances under another pseudonym. Three is her lucky number; she has three daughters, and the events in her life have always been in threes. "I love writing for Silhouette," Cait says. "One of the best perks about all this hard work is the thrilling reader response and the warm, snug sense that I have given readers an enjoyable, entertaining gift."

The Women of Freedom Valley
Montana, 1882

Magda Claas   **Fleur Arnaud**   **Anatasia Duscha**   **Beatrice Avril**   **Jasmine Dupree**

Anna Claas m. Paul Bennett

Tanner Bennett

Kylie Bennett

Miranda Bennett

Cynthia Whitehall China Belle Ruppurt Fancy Benjamin Margaret Gertraud LaRue

AN INVITATION FROM CAIT LONDON

I invite you to step into my brand-new series,
FREEDOM VALLEY. I hope you enjoy *Last Dance,* the first of
this series. The town, Freedom, is just as picturesque as the
valley, packed with everything a small town usually has—
except its traditions.

Set in Montana, the series is based on women of the
1880s who came together for protection. Back then, men
desiring wives had to present themselves according to the
Rules of Courting and the traditions those independent women
established. Contemporary males, including the Bachelor Club,
chafe at the rules, but The Women's Council intends to keep
those traditions.

In *Last Dance,* a Freedom Valley tradition, you'll get a good
taste of what is to come as we visit each family established by
those Founding Mothers.

See you in Freedom Valley—

Cait London

Prologue

———

Town of Freedom, 1882
From the journal of Magda Claas

We named our valley Freedom, and our town, too. There were ten of us at first, that hot, dry summer of 1881. We found ourselves by chance, gathered in a small beautiful valley, sharing what we had to survive. Beautiful, snowcapped mountains soared along one side of the valley and there was a lovely lake and lush wild grass for our stock. We came from all parts of the world, women with children, women who had lost families and who had seen the darker side of life. Fleur Arnaud, unmarried, had lost a child by a man who took her against her will. Anatasia Duscha's husband and son died in the wars. Beatrice Avril was a bondwoman, preyed upon by men for her pretty looks and dainty ways. Jasmine Du-

pree, full with child, had come from the poor South. Cynthia Whitehall came from Boston for freedom her family would not give. China Belle Ruppurt had run from buffalo hunters who had used her poorly. Fancy Benjamin's father sold her to a farmer for a sack of oats, and widowed Margaret Gertraud's breads and rolls didn't save her or her children from thieves who took everything and left them starving. We know little about the woman called LaRue, except that she had loved and lost.

Magda Claas is my name, and I know how to work. I want a man, the man I choose for a husband, not to see me as a cow in the field or a servant, but as a woman with a heart and pride. I wish to be treated gently, as I have seen men honor their wives. At the end of the day, I crochet lace with needle and thread, and dream of the man I will accept into my heart.

What a strange mix we were, some of us with children clinging to our skirts, or nursing at our breasts. All ten of us without men and not caring much for those that came calling with crude ways.

We wanted to choose our lives, and so it was that day with rawhide men and drovers and rapscallions circling us, that we decided to act. By the end of summer, we knew what we had to do to live as we wished, as we dreamed, and so we made our laws for men who came wife-hunting.

We were not helpless women to be preyed upon by these rough men. Each of us knew how to protect ourselves, and together we were strong as a family.

So it was that we decided to come together, farmers and mothers and women with pasts. We became a community of women who helped each other, governed by the Women's Council. For we would be free women, to set the rules of how we should be treated as wives. For be it known, that to take a dear wife from our circle, the husband-candidate will have to follow our rules and customs, abide with those rules in the marriage, passing our inspection. Else there would be no marriages or wife-taking in Freedom. We stand together in this, women deciding to marry as we wish, protected by our sisterhood.

Magda Claas, Midwife and Healer and Butter Maker
Town of Freedom, Freedom Valley
Montana Territory, July 1882

One

They were sweet back then, an eight-year-old boy and a four-year-old girl. Tanner had placed his baseball bat aside to fix her wagon's bent wheel. While Gwyneth clearly adored him, he acted all gruff with his friends riding their bicycles up the road. He made yucking noises when she kissed him on the cheek, but he'll grow up to be a fine man, just as loving and good as his dad. One day, he'll know his love and he'll come courting according to the rules of Freedom Valley.

—From the journal of Anna Bennett, descendant of Magda Claas and the mother of Tanner Bennett.

Tanner Bennett expertly knelt on his mother's roof and tore away the damaged shingles. Familiar to his hand, his father's hammer was worn, a contrast to the new shingles he'd just patched into the old.

He inhaled Montana's midmorning April air, and knew that his ex-wife would soon come calling to warn him off. He'd known Gwyneth all her life, and he sensed from the dark look she burned at him in the café that she wanted to set down her rules.

Too bad. He had rules of his own now, and he wasn't feeling friendly.

From the top of the two-story home, he scanned the small rural town he'd left eighteen years ago. Nestled in Freedom Valley, a lush valley blanketed with fields and cattle and cradled by soaring, snowcapped mountains, Freedom—the town—was quiet. Down the country road that led to town, babies were napping, housewives were cleaning, store clerks were waiting on customers, and the café crowd was gossiping over morning coffee. Freedom Valley hadn't changed. Birthed by single women united for their protection in the 1880s, their traditions remained in their descendants. Lives and families blended through the years, the descendants' colorful names proudly stamped with immigrant heritage, biblical reference and popular contemporary ones. The town's square was lined by two-story buildings, little changed since Montana's cattle-drive days.

In the distance, just past pickup trucks lined around the feed store, and up the street from the florist, his mother rested in a tiny, well-tended cemetery. An auto accident had taken her life too soon—on a fog-draped country highway, Anna never saw the semitruck at the highway intersection. Beside her grave lay Paul Bennett's, her husband, victim of a heart attack when Tanner was only twelve.

At thirty-six now, Tanner felt old memories rustle to

life, the slight breeze stirring the leaves of an oak tree nearby, while sunlight danced upon Anna Bennett's beloved home. Not far from town, the twenty-acre farm was neat from the chicken house to the pasture to the vegetable garden. In Anna's sunporch, the impatiens and tomato plants she'd started from seed waited to be put into her gardens. Tiny feed-store sacks of lettuce, green beans and cucumber seed lay in a neat row as if she couldn't wait to plant them.

Tanner scrubbed his hand across the aching tightness within his bare chest. In the six weeks since her death, he'd cleared away his business commitments on the Northwest Pacific coast—building handcrafted, custom-order, wooden fishing boats had suited him. In his absence, a good friend would handle his business there.

Tanner scanned the small farm and wondered how his widowed mother had managed her young brood, to see them safely into their lives. He'd come back to visit his mother through the years, but what held her here, in this tiny place? Anna Bennett never complained through her hardships. What was the source of her strength? What gave her such peace?

Peace. Would he ever find peace?

The church's white spire shot into the clear blue Montana sky. Twelve years ago, he'd been married there, a young man with his blushing, sweet bride tucked against his side, heading off into a bright new future away from Freedom.

But that first night, Gwyneth Smith Bennett had been terrified, running from him, and despite his determination and patience, the marriage ended—*without consummation.*

A white panel van soared into Anna's driveway. Scrawled along the side, a purple and pink Gwen's Pots announced his ex-wife—information mischievously tossed at him by Willa, owner of Willa's Wagon Wheel Café, and incumbent mayor of Freedom. According to Leonard at the gas station, Gwen's van got good mileage, needed a tuneup and so did she.

One week in Freedom's close-knit community provided more information than he'd wanted about his ex-wife—not that he'd asked. In a small town, lives weren't that private.

His hand stilled over his heart, the one she'd torn to shreds years ago. He'd rebuilt his life without her, and he regretted the momentary sharp clench of pain that just looking at her could bring.

When a man's pride was badly stomped by a woman, he wasn't likely to forget.

Tanner inhaled sharply as she stepped briskly out of the van, her short blond hair gleaming in the sun. She looked like a boy, not a thirty-two-year-old woman, until he took in that compact, curved body. Gwyneth Smith Bennett, dressed in a T-shirt and cutoff bib overalls that showed off the tanned length of her legs above her practical work boots, wasn't happy. Her scowl shot around Anna's untended herbal and vegetable gardens, the sheds and the chicken house to the small field bordering the Smith ranch. She swung open the gate of the white picket fence and glanced at a large branch, broken free by the storm, on the freshly cut lawn. Then she marched up the stone walkway, usually bordered by summer flowers, past the new green starts of the yellow and red Dutch tulip bed, past the concrete birdbath filled with leaves and up onto the front porch, out of Tanner's sight. The old brass door knocker sounded briskly and then Gwyneth appeared, marching around the side of the two-story house.

"Oh, Gwynnie…" he called lightly from the rooftop, unable to resist the tease of long ago.

She stopped in midstep and her face jerked upward. Stark in the bright sunlight, Gwyneth's expression tightened into a scowl. The woman's face had been honed from the girl's that he had loved and married—*had he really loved her? Or had he wanted to protect her from her overbearing and possessive father?*

No, it was more than that, and he'd paid a heavy price.

Gwyneth's mouth tightened—he remembered instantly how sweet that little cupid bow tasted all those years ago—perfect and virginal. Now, her hazel eyes weren't happily filled with him, and beneath those dark arching eyebrows, brilliant anger lashed at him. The peach-gold skin across her cheekbones gleamed, her expression darkening. In her dark mood, her jaw had the locked set of old Leather's, her father. Without missing a beat, she moved to the wooden ladder he'd braced against the house, walked it backward and let it drop to the grass.

"When are you leaving? It isn't soon enough," she shot up to him, her hands braced on her waist.

Tanner settled back on his haunches; the furious woman on the ground below. While visiting Anna, he'd met her accidentally several times; they hadn't spoken, an icy mountain of pain and anger standing between them. He didn't like the ugly fury within him at first, and later a cold distance seemed safer. This lean and shapely woman little resembled the frightened twenty-year-old girl who had run from their first night as husband and wife. He'd never forget the sight of her as he walked to their bed in that hotel—wide-eyed fear that had eventually ended a marriage never begun. They were both older now, and he wasn't letting her push him. At one time, he'd been very careful of her; but that time was gone. "I'll leave when I'm ready."

"I hear down at Livingston's Hardware that you're fixing up Anna's place to sell. I suppose you'll be leaving, going back to your big Northwest Pacific coast custom-made fishing boat business, right?"

Apparently, the gossips had been working Gwyneth, too. Her eyes flashed with an impatience and anger that was new to Tanner. "I'm flattered that you're interested in my life, Gwynnie."

"Do not call me 'Gwynnie.' I'm not six anymore and I don't have a crush on you any longer. I'm not interested in anything about you. I just want you out of town. You came back a week ago, and the gossip is already flying. I can't walk down the street without someone mentioning that you're back in town and looking at me as if they expect—well, never mind. This is my town. I've stayed. I haven't been heading off for college, or teaching in Kansas City, or traveling around the world in the merchant marine. I've stayed right here and took care of Pop and now that he's gone, I'm running the ranch. It won't work with the both of us here, not with what everybody knows about—"

"Our marriage? The one that never actually took place?" Tanner fought the stirring of old frustration and anger—a young bridegroom set on his wedding night and a frightened runaway bride made for lasting and ugly memories. He'd never hurt her, never gave her reason to fear— He'd tried for three years while he was teaching in Kansas City to disarm Gwyneth's fear of him, to make her see how much he loved her. But distance, time and her coldness eventually made him agree to a divorce. At the time, Gwyneth wanted a divorce, rather than an annulment—she couldn't bear for the town gossips to know that they'd never consummated their marriage, that she was too terrified at the sight of him to—

His stomach clenched as he remembered young Gwyneth's horrified expression, the way she'd run out of the hotel and home to her father.

Old "Leather" Smith had reveled in proof that he was right, that Tanner wasn't suitable for his only daughter. Leather hadn't wanted to give up his daughter, who was also his ranch hand, cook and cleaning woman; the bully had wanted to own Gwyneth, not to free her to a life of her own, and had blocked Tanner's attempts to win back his wife.

She tensed, then swept her hand aside, dismissing his taunt. "You are going to stay up on that roof until I make you see sense."

"Oh, really?" Tanner asked before he reached over to an upstairs window and jerked it open. After baring his teeth in a cold smile, Tanner entered the window. With every step down the stairs and out on the porch and around the house, he thought about the woman demanding that he leave Freedom.

When he stood facing Gwyneth—so close he noted that she barely reached his shoulder—he asked the question that had been burning him. "Why did you keep my name, Gwyneth?"

Color rose in her cheeks and her hazel eyes darkened into green as she looked up those inches to meet his gaze. Tanner tensed as her eyes ripped down his six-foot-three body, heated a path across his shoulders and blinked several times at his bare chest. For a heartbeat, her eyes widened in fear, quickly shielded. The shiver that ran down her body was enough to make Tanner clench his fists, slapped by the nightmare of their wedding night. Then she stepped back from him, lifted her chin and squared her shoulders. "You know why I kept the Bennett name. I loved Anna, and it kept her close, as though she was the mother I never had. I liked having her name. And an annulment would have...would have created even more gossip."

"It's *my* name, and you took it." A dark ridge of anger leaped upon Tanner, and he shoved it down, just as he had all those years ago. "Old Leather created plenty of gossip all by himself. My mother didn't like hearing that I'd mistreated you that night and that you ran back to him to be safe."

Gwyneth had remained his wife, in his heart, for years, and now that same tearing away of his heart began, just looking at her.

"Your mother called him out one night and stuck a berry pie in his hand. Whatever she said to him made him angry and made him stop those rumors. He ate the pie, but he wasn't happy. He respected her...everyone did. She came to see him as he was dying and helped me with the funeral six years ago." Her gaze shifted to the lily of the valley bed that would soon bloom. "I'm sorry about Pop's stories. I tried to stop him. Anna knew the truth and she was a good woman. She had a peace that gentled everyone around her."

"She did at that. She raised Kylie and Miranda and myself without help and was never bitter or afraid. She loved this valley and she brought a good deal of the babies here into the world." Why had his mother loved the town so deeply? Why had she clung to the traditions begun by those frontier women? What was Anna Bennett's secret of life, always seeing the good in people where none could be found? Where was the peace she had found? Where was his own?

He had to kill whatever ran through him for his ex-wife. He had to start a new life; he wanted a home and children and peace. Tanner frowned down at Gwyneth, his memories running like scars across his heart because of this woman. She'd colored relationships with other women, ruining them, for he could never find the right taste, or the same fascination.

Gwyneth ran her hand through her cropped hair, spiking it and sunlight danced across the tips. "I saw Kylie and Miranda at the funeral. I was hoping one of them—"

Tanner propped the ladder against the house again. He traced the path of white-rumped antelope leaping from the cattle fields off into the woods. His sisters couldn't bear to dismantle the house, to take one doily from Anna's home, and the job was left to him. Tanner had repaired the house since he was twelve, taking the place of his carpenter father in more ways than one. His steadfast, loving mother had been a miracle and a source of strength to those she touched, but not for Anna or anyone else was he moving to Gwyneth's wishes. "Take your hopes somewhere else," he said. "I'm not going anywhere until I'm ready."

"You're not small town makings. You've been all over the world. You don't belong here. I do—" she began firmly.

He noted the tiny gold studs in her ears. She must have defied old Leather; he wouldn't have liked the "silly beautifications." A bitter taste of memory tightened Tanner's mouth. She hadn't stepped out from Leather's care years ago, when Tanner had been desperate to reason with her. "You wanted a divorce and not an annulment. I agreed to that farce and that's the last agreeing I do with you."

"It is hard, Tanner Bennett, to believe that you are sweet Anna's son. I'll be glad when you sell this place and—"

"Don't count on it," Tanner said slowly, feeling the burn of old wounds and the need to cut at the woman who had stolen his life, his dreams. He could have tried to fill himself with other dreams, another woman, but life hadn't turned that way for Tanner Bennett. Within himself, in the deep dark certain truth of his life, he knew that he'd have to find peace as his mother had.

Her eyes widened, sunlight glistening on her lashes. "But at the hardware store, they said that you and your sisters would probably sell. It's a wonderful house with a few acres. I'd buy it myself, if I could afford it—just because I want to hold Anna close—"

"You think *I* don't want to hold my mother close?" he demanded curtly. Tanner didn't like thinking about another family in Anna's home, or on her land. He wasn't ready to let her go yet, the house still filled with her scent and memories squeezing him too hard to move on. He'd come to the funeral and with his sisters sat in Anna's house later, a part of their lives torn away by death, each feeling guilty for not visiting more. Agreeing to temporarily leave Anna's home as it was, they each went back to their lives far away.

Now Tanner had come back, needing to find peace with his mother's passing, and with his life. He remembered all they didn't have, all that they did have because of Anna's hard work and her endless patience and love. "She should have had more. Life was too hard for her."

Gwyneth's hazel eyes softened, drifting over Anna's house snuggled into shady trees, herbs and flower beds.

"You were there for her, and Kylie and Miranda. Her children were her life."

"She worked too hard." Tanner noted the bitterness in his tone, the sharp echo of pain in his heart. A widow, bearing the hardships of raising her family, Anna never wavered in helping others and always with a tender smile.

Because the tilt of Gwyneth's head as she studied him brought back a sweet memory, he brushed his thumb across the corner of her mouth. He noted the fine pink surface, void of lipstick. How long had he wanted her? Since he was eighteen and she was fourteen? Or years before that, when she'd come crying from Leather's jibes into his mother's arms?

"So how's it going, Gwynnie?" he asked to taunt the woman who had just paled at his touch and to derail the sweet memories before that fateful wedding night.

She shivered with anger, her eyes biting at him. "If you bring a hussy into Anna's house, I'll be all over you."

"My, my, my," he drawled, and grinned at her, pleased that he could rev her so easily, this woman who had torn apart his young dreams. Young Gwyneth had been sweet and retiring and this one wasn't. "You certainly have a high opinion of me."

She impatiently ran her hand through her short hair, and he remembered his fingers wrapped deep in the silky sunlight of her long hair. Clearly trying to maintain control, Gwyneth slashed a dark look up at him. "I mean it, Tanner. You bring a woman into Anna's house and she wouldn't like that."

"A woman? Like a woman in my bed? All hot and bothered and—" He couldn't resist teasing Gwyneth, or was he? That night, long ago, had ripped away part of him. At first he'd tried to make love with other women, and he'd tried to make relationships work—but somehow he couldn't forget that night.

"You know what I mean about women," she shot back at him, narrowing her sight on the earring in his ear as though it marked him as "sinner" and "lech." "You've probably...I've heard about sailors in port... how they—"

"Yes?" he drawled, really enjoying Gwyneth's obvious impression of his years away from Freedom Valley.

The quick color moving up her cheeks pleased him. He lifted an eyebrow, fascinated with the woman scowling up at him. Years ago, Gwyneth was little more than a sweet shadow, a girl on the cusp of being a woman—fragile, quiet, uncertain and yet just as fascinating with her green-brown eyes, her cupid's-bow mouth, those dimples in her cheeks. He ran his hand across her hair, riffling the short strands. "You look good with short hair."

He took in the length of her fit, athletic body. Gwyneth worked hard and the muscles were smoothly defined on her arms and legs. She had the look of a strong earthy, sensual woman who could take as well as give...not the kind to lie quiet beneath a man. Tanner pushed down that bit of nudging lust for his ex-wife. "Goes with the rest of you."

She flushed and looked away, and came back with a haughty "It's practical. A gentleman would put on a shirt while holding a discussion with a lady."

"Don't count on manners from me, Gwyneth Bennett," he said slowly, meaning it. Once again, he remembered her expression as he walked toward her on their wedding night—her eyes had skimmed his chest in that same fearful way…and she'd run away.

Gwyneth had taken his pride and his dreams that night, and now she deserved nothing.

Her indrawn breath hissed in the sweetly scented morning and she paled. "And don't you dare turn this into a boy's clubhouse with all your old buddies. They're all here or come back periodically, all your old high school football and sports buddies—Gabriel Deerhorn, though he keeps to his mountains most of the time—Michael Cusack, York, Frazier, and the rest of your swaggering Bachelor Club! Any beer and babe parties in Anna's house and I'll call any wives attached to them. If they're not married, I'll call their mothers, and Kylie and Miranda, and I'll bring you up before the Women's Council as an undesirable influence on married and unmarried men. They still remember when you pierced your ear and the Bachelor Club, your swaggering boys' club, followed suit—every last one… Just get out of town and make it easy on everyone."

"I don't like threats and I'll decide when I'm leaving." Tanner didn't like the too-soft snarl to his tone, because that proved she was getting to him. He'd honored his mother his entire life, respected her home; Gwyneth's low-dog opinion of him nettled.

"Good…decide to leave quick, and I don't make threats. I make promises, and try not to embarrass your family when you go sniffing after women." With that, Gwyneth lifted her chin and tromped back around Anna's house. Gwyneth slammed the door of her van and it roared away. Tanner realized darkly that her threat was the first he'd ever heard from her. His shy, sweet bride of years ago was nothing like the fast-mouthed, hot-tempered woman this morning.

Did it really matter? Tanner wondered bleakly. Why should he care if Gwyneth had threatened him with the worst fate of an unmarried male in Freedom Valley?

He followed the van hurling down Anna's dirt driveway and out onto the unpaved road leading to the Smith ranch. Across the green patchwork of fields, he turned to view Freedom, a quaint town with a tall white church steeple—where he'd married Gwyneth. Then his view swept the town with its neat, well-tended houses and stores, its town square, cherished by the community and where the spit-and-whittle "boys" of eighty or so, held their meetings.

He inhaled slowly; after eighteen years of intermittent visits, he'd come back to the valley's traditions and an ex-wife's threat—*"I'll bring you up before the Women's Council as an undesirable influence on married and unmarried men…"*

Freedom's Women's Council was powerful, a tradition established from the single women settlers looking for husbands. Women who would choose their own paths, they'd had to protect themselves from brutish men and had formed a family of women, sisters bonded together. Traditional approval of the council usually meant a smooth courtship, according to the women's terms. The man seeking a bride had to conform to the various stages set forth by the Women's Council, and a century and more later, this approval was held dear by families and prospective brides.

A man marked as a "Cull" or reject by the Women's Council could court, but he'd have a difficult time, because his beloved would want the same courtly traditions as her friends. An unhappy prospective bride could make her lover quite uncomfortable.

And so it was that most men in and around Freedom

Valley abided by the *Women's Council's Rules for Bride Courting,* an 1880s manual fiercely defended by all the women in the area—mothers, daughters, sisters and aunts. Life in Freedom Valley could become quite challenging for males not abiding by the Rules for Bride Courting.

Consequently the friends of a misbehaving "Cull" were likely to be in for trouble, too, outcasts in the dating game, and the wheels of romance could come to a frustrating, cold stop.

After his wedding night fiasco, Tanner knew about frustrating, cold stops. In his haste to claim Gwyneth, Tanner had shoved aside traditions—

He rubbed his callused hands over his face, pushing away memories and the unexpected, uncomfortable emotions circling him about Gwyneth. With a sigh, Tanner went into his mother's house and sat in the neat, cheery kitchen. A cobweb she would have never allowed taunted him with memories.

Just finished with college and with a new teaching job far away, he'd wanted Gwyneth to marry him quickly— *"A girl like Gwyneth has a lot to fight,"* his mother had said all those years ago, standing up on a chair to dust away an encroaching cobweb. *"Her mother died when she was two and Leather hasn't made her life easy, treating her more like a possession than a daughter—a hardworking ranch hand was how he treated her. Now you're pushing her. Give her more time...let her come to her own decisions, in her own time."*

But twelve years ago, time had run out, and so had his bride. Tanner slammed his palm down on the table, jarring the mug and coffee that had grown cold. He picked up the framed picture of a beaming, eager groom and a blushing bride on the church's front steps, studied it for a heartbeat, then slammed it facedown on Anna's practical tablecloth.

"Don't worry, Mother," he said grimly to the empty kitchen. "I'm not in the market for another bloodletting."

Gwyneth leaped from her van and ran up to the old weathered house with its missing shingles and battered flooring and leaky plumbing. Fumbling with her keys, she quickly clicked open the series of locks on the door, and stepped inside the hallway. She slammed the door on the sunshine that had moments ago gleamed on Tanner's black waving hair, on that expanse of deeply tanned skin across his chest and the light matting of hair Veeing down into his low-slung jeans.

That shaggy haircut, the black strands damp upon his face and neck, did little to proclaim him a gentleman. The scowl that drew his eyebrows together was too fierce for Anna's son and the set of his mouth said he wasn't handing out favors. *"I don't like threats and I'll decide when I'm leaving."*

One look at Tanner, and buried emotions had hit her like a firestorm. She hadn't intended to stop at Anna's, to blast Tanner, but delivering her pottery to Freedom's Decor Shop and buying feed for the ranch had drawn Tanner-is-back comments from everyone she'd met. It was how they looked at her, that curious hopeful romantic look that brought back that night and how she'd run from him. He'd never hurt her and yet, she couldn't bear for him to touch her— She should have known…

Sucking in air, listening to the furious pounding of her heart, she flattened her body back against the hallway's ancient faded wallpaper.

"Hello, Gwynnie," he'd called from Anna's rooftop.

He'd looked so powerful then, scowling down at her, his body solid from hard work, his big hands broad and rough. His mouth turned into a fierce, grim line, black eyes burning her, tearing through her body. After all those years, his anger was still there, lashing at her.

She'd adored him all her life. He'd been a high school football hero, grabbing a scholarship and soaring away to college in another state. He came home that summer, just after her high school graduation. He'd tilted his head as he looked at her and smiled slowly, as she blushed. "Hello, Gwynnie," he'd said softly, tugging on her braids, and had asked for a date.

She was frightened then—she'd never had a date, her father wouldn't let her, and somehow Tanner had understood. The next morning, he'd crossed the fence separating Anna's land from the Smith ranch and walked to her father's stalled old tractor. By late afternoon, the tractor was purring, Tanner was plowing, and old Leather was swearing, nettled by Tanner's "I'll take good care of Gwyneth. If you have no objections, I'd like to take her to a movie, sir."

Old Leather, a man who craved respect, had gone down easily.

Then suddenly, they were dating and laughing and playing, and she was floating on air. Tanner's kisses were steamy, his body taut and hot, but cherishing her, he had wanted to wait. He wanted to start a beautiful life with a perfect marriage. Two more years passed and then Tanner had graduated, ready to take a teaching job far away and he wanted her with him.

Confident in their love and future, he had pushed her to marry him, arguing fiercely with Leather that she was twenty and ready to be Tanner's wife. Fearing the loss of his daughter and ranch hand and cook, Leather had dug in, snarling and resenting the younger man. But she hadn't cared about his grumbling; she'd wanted to be with Tanner. She'd never been anywhere, but she was in love and so ready. She hadn't minded that they hadn't courted according to Freedom Valley's century-old customs, she'd wanted Tanner too much.

Had she loved him? She'd worshiped him, adored him, waited for the sight of him. But what did she know of love at twenty? Was she only looking for freedom from a father who demanded too much?

After the wedding, she was terrified; she held tightly against her new groom at the church, his body pressing against hers. That first night, with the new marriage certificate resting beside the bed and Tanner's ring on her finger, she couldn't stop the clenched-tight fear. She'd trembled as Tanner had walked toward the bed, a towel around his hips....

Penny's whining and scratching at the front door cut through the terrifying memory and Gwyneth let the German shepherd into the house. Darker and more sturdily built than his mate, Rolf pushed through the door for an ear-scratching.

Gwyneth tried to stop the twelve-year-old echo—his voice had been unsteady, frustrated—"Gwyneth, I won't hurt you. Don't back away from me. Look, we won't do anything tonight, okay? You're tired—all that wedding stuff. We'll just sleep and everything will be better in the morning...."

But it wasn't, because she couldn't bear to think of him holding her, his big powerful body invading her body—

Later, when he'd come to the Smith ranch house and tried to talk with her, she couldn't bear to face him. Tanner came from a loving family and he deserved children; she couldn't bear for him to touch her—not that intimate way. While they were dating, Tanner had been so gentle and proper, his kisses and light caresses so sweet that she'd hoped—

But the old fear remained firmly embedded and on her wedding night, she'd run crying to her father. He was happy, crowing about how right he'd been, that she and Tanner weren't "a mix." She hadn't returned Tanner's calls, except the one message two years later that had asked for an annulment—she couldn't have that and he'd agreed to a divorce.

"He just lives five miles down the country road to Anna's, and the Bennett property borders mine. The rumors will be flying in no time—" She pointed a stern finger at both well-trained guard dogs. "Do not become friends with Tanner Bennett. Don't hurt him, but don't go wagging your tails for a new friend, either," she amended.

Then pushing her hands through her hair and her memories of Tanner away, Gwyneth took a deep breath. "No one is going to fix that rotten fence post but me, or repair that hose on the tractor, or tag the ears of those new calves, so I'd better get after it."

She ignored the ringing telephone; she wasn't in the mood for anyone reminding her that Tanner had returned to town, living not far away. She pointed her finger down the hallway, directing the dogs to hunt through the house for unwelcome intruders. The dogs were not only her friends, but her protectors. One sound from them would tell her of danger.

She paused and jerked open a drawer on the hallway table. Her unframed wedding picture and the simple gold ring rolling across it mocked her. She flipped the picture over and shoved the drawer closed, just as she would any thoughts of Tanner. "I am a woman now, not a twenty-year-old, lovesick girl, high on the town hero," she said to the pale woman in the mirror. "I've got responsibilities and work to do, and Tanner will move on. He'll get bored with small town life, and he'll leave."

Then her thoughts ran across the worn linoleum at her feet, like worrying mice that would not go away.

Why hadn't he married? Why hadn't he filled another woman's body with his babies? What would have happened had they courted in the way most women of Freedom cherished, and she'd trusted him with her secret?

Two

Not all men have good hearts, and that is why the Founding Mothers of Freedom Valley decided to lay out their terms when men came courting. I do not like the rage that burns in my heart now, for someone I love has been hurt and I am powerless to avenge her.

—Anna Bennett

Gwyneth dragged herself from under the tractor and wiped her greasy hands on a rag. She swished the barn's straw from the backside of her cutoff bib overalls, and stood snarling at the metal monster she'd coaxed to life. She hated the old tractor with all her soul; the unsteady feral growling noises provided frustration relief, curling around the airy old barn. She flopped on her baseball hat and damned Tanner Bennett for making her lose a precious night's sleep. Yesterday, Tanner had invaded her life, her nightmares. She didn't want to remember him at all, not the tender way he'd kissed her back then, nor the pain and frustration in his expression that night and all the other times he'd tried to call or talk to her.

She'd hurt him badly, and yesterday his scars were showing. Tanner wasn't the sweetheart she'd known. The lines across his broad forehead and the crinkling at the corner of his eyes told of hours in the weather. She could almost smell the salt air upon him, the nuances of foreign lands and experience with women. Clean-cut Tanner of years ago was now a man with dark, sultry eyes and broad, powerful shoulders that she wanted to—

She shook her head. No man should have such a flat ridged stomach, narrow hips and long, powerful legs. His worn deck shoes marked his experiences away from Freedom Valley and from her. His body, though still lean, was that of a workman…corded, solid and sending out restless vibrations to hers. Tanner had always preferred action to paperwork and there was a hard, fierce look about him, his shields raised. His dislike of her had draped around her like a heavy, cold cloak.

"Swaggering, arrogant—" she muttered, then a flash of a younger, boyish Tanner, clad in his football armor and winking at her, set her heart tumbling. She didn't want to remember how he had looked all those years ago, walking toward her, dark eyes gleaming, the night of the Sweetheart Dance. She was just eighteen and it was the first time Tanner had taken her to a dance. She'd been thrilled, freed from her father, filled with summer's sweet expectations and wearing her first dressy dress, borrowed from Kylie. Tanner had taken her in his arms for the last dance, and she'd felt he was taking her in his arms for a lifetime—

Now, she shivered, mentally tearing herself away from that sweet moment years ago. She'd made a life she could live and without her father's steady demands, she found peace in a hard day's work and long, quiet hours at her wheel. She missed Leather, of course, because despite his stingy, hard ways, she was his daughter and loved him. But Anna had been the mother she'd never known—sweet, loving Anna, who understood her fears and always offered a comforting cup of herbal tea....

Gwyneth slashed her forearm across her face, the flannel wiping away the tears. She swallowed and straightened with the resolve that had served her through the years of keeping the Smith ranch, of paying her father's medical bills. Dew hung on the pasture, and mist layered the morning. Somehow she'd work and manage as she always had...and then Tanner would be gone. He'd only come to set his mother's house aright, a sad obligation; then he'd be off to a life far from Freedom Valley. She had only to wait. She'd coolly smile at the town's friendly nudges toward her ex-husband, keep quiet, and mind her own business.

"Oh my, he's a handsome man. He's got those wide shoulders and that seaman's walk and he's sweet just like Anna. I see her in him," Willa at the café had said, taking the fresh eggs from Gwyneth. "I'm glad you're keeping Anna's chickens. She would have liked that, because she clearly loved you like a daughter."

Yesterday, Tanner's dislike of her, a woman who had run from her marriage bed and shivered in fear, was as clear as the wide blue Montana sky. His scowl had turned into a wicked, taunting grin because he knew the truth of their wedding night and the consummation that

never took place. It was their secret that he could hold
and twist and torment— *"Oh, Gwynnie…"*

She hated him for that—for holding a part of her life
that she'd shared with no one, except his mother. But
Tanner didn't know the reason she fled that night and
she wouldn't give that to him, too. She'd told her deepest
fears and the reasons for them to Anna, who had held
her as she'd cried.

She had work to do, a ranch to tend, and pots to make
and none of that required any thought of an ex-husband.
There in the shadows of the barn, the cats daintily licking at the fresh creamy milk she'd given them, Gwyneth
kicked the tractor's tire again. She was in an evil, dark
mood and Tanner was the cause of her missing sleep.
As she had done for years, she threw out her hands and
released the biggest yell possible, stirring the swallows
in the rafters. With a quick, tight, satisfied smile that her
frustration release technique had worked, she jerked the
leather gloves from her back pocket, jamming them onto
her hands.

A sharp, happy bark whipped her head around to the
doorway, where the intruder stood. She couldn't see his
face, but the tall, powerful lines of his body said Tanner
had come to call, Penny and Rolf nuzzling against his
hands. "Get off my land, Tanner," she snapped, walking
toward him.

There was no Leather to stand between them now, no
sweet Anna to help soothe the rough edges of her fears.
Time had changed Gwyneth, for now she wanted to deal
with that nasty mood prowling between them. She'd
been in control of her life before he'd come back and
she'd liked her freedom; she wouldn't have another man
pulling her strings by anger or by love. "Penny. Rolf.

Down,'' Gwyneth ordered and immediately the dogs sat by Tanner.

''You yelled?'' he asked in an overpolite tone. ''You seem to like doing that.'' In the misty morning, his hair was damp and waving, his jaw dark with stubble. His mouth was set in the same unforgiving grim line as yesterday, but today fury burned his deep-set eyes. The black sweatshirt he wore emphasized his dangerous look, his worn jeans and work boots damp with dew from his walk to her house. ''You should answer your telephone, Gwyneth. I didn't like your little visit yesterday. It wasn't polite. I thought I'd repay the favor and even the score.''

She cut her hand across a layer of cool mist, tearing away the cobweb tenderness of the past. ''There is no score between us. I stay on my land and you're trespassing, Bennett.''

''You're in a nasty mood, Mrs. Bennett. Had a good night's sleep, did you?'' he asked in a dark, pleasant tone that lifted the hairs on her nape. The name Bennett slapped her, accused her.

''Did you?'' she tossed back; she had no guilt to spare for him. Gwyneth resented looking up those inches to his face, resented the tremor that went through her, the memories that had been safely tucked away slashing at her.

He handed her a note written by Anna. ''This was by her telephone.''

The note read: ''Call Gwyneth. Ask her to plow my garden.''

Gwyneth fought the hot burn of her tears, carefully folding the note and tucking it into her bib overalls pocket; she'd read it again later, treasuring a woman she loved. "I usually do that for her. That was six weeks ago...."

"You never plowed it." Tanner's voice was angry, biting her, condemning her. His gaze slashed the corral gate, hanging from one hinge, the unpainted house and the assortment of old farm equipment rusting in the field. "You're killing yourself on this place. You've got guard dogs—trained guard dogs—four locks on the front and back doors, and you're..."

His lips clamped on the rest and he scowled at her. "I want this cleaned up. I'm not going anywhere soon and I don't want you tearing into my mother's driveway again for a kamikaze attack. You're working too hard," he added more softly, watching her too intently, as though he could see where the darkness tore at her.

"Ranch work is hard. It's my land now and I'm keeping it. Fences don't mend themselves, you know, and cattle still have to be fed in the winter, when a blizzard comes through."

Tanner slammed his open hand against the weathered barn boards. "Don't hand me that. You're still terrified of men—or is it just me? Everything was fine until that night—you were a bit pale and jittery looking, but innocent brides-to-be are known to be— What happened to you, Gwyneth?"

"Lay off," she said, brushing by him and slapping her bare thigh for her dogs to follow. Penny and Rolf remained at Tanner's boots, tongues hanging out as they grinned, their tails happily thumping the ground.

She slapped her bare thigh again, impatiently this time, and Tanner's easy smile wasn't nice. "We've become friends. As soon as your van leaves, they both run to mother's house. They each have a bowl at her back steps and I just continued to feed them as she had done.

They are trained guard dogs and I want to know why. Invite me in and we'll chat. Just to set the rules. Unless you're afraid.''

Afraid? When had she not been afraid? Gwyneth tried to ignore the pounding of her heart and fought back to when she hadn't been afraid—she hadn't been afraid of Tanner and Leather was a man others feared, keeping her safe. Then just before the wedding, her life had changed. "I'm not afraid of anything," she lied.

"Well, then, you won't be afraid to invite me in for a neighborly chat, will you?"

"You're nosing around here, just for the sheer nastiness of it. Anna wouldn't have liked that."

He looked down at her, and for a heartbeat, the hard line of his mouth softened. "Are you getting all steamed up to yell again, Gwynnie?"

"Anna wouldn't have wanted you bothering me," she restated firmly.

"Don't hide behind my mother. Don't ever hide from me behind anyone again," he said, reminding her of how she'd hovered behind Leather, afraid to talk with the husband she abandoned on their wedding night.

"I can handle you on my own," she answered, lifting her chin to angle a hard stare up at him.

"Can you?" The question was too soft as Tanner reached out, grabbed the flannel shirt covering her T-shirt and hauled her up close to him. Fear ruling her, Gwyneth brought her boot down on his and there in the quiet layers of morning mist, with the meadowlark trilling on the old fence post and the roosters crowing, Tanner studied her face. "I'm wearing steel toe work boots, honey. I never felt a thing. Now that was an interesting move. You've had some self-defense training, too, haven't you? Why?"

Her hands had sought an anchor as he'd lifted her to her tiptoes, and the warm muscles surging on his upper arms told her that Tanner had only gotten stronger. She met his dark look, forced her fingers to uncurl from his arms and pushed the trembling fear back in its hole.

"The Founding Mothers knew how to shoot well enough to protect themselves and others. Times haven't changed that much, just a new twist on the methods," she shot back and tore herself free of him. She breathed unsteadily, trying to recover her reality before Tanner began prying into her life, yet every breath took his scent into her.

"Not around here. That's what the video training course was at my mother's, wasn't it? She was helping you. Why?"

She missed Anna terribly. "We were friends. I loved her. She helped me...we learned self-defense together. That's all you need to know."

"My mother? Sparring in the backyard?" he asked in disbelief.

His expression was dazed, almost comical and Gwyneth waded in to deepen the shock and shake his almighty arrogance. Apparently Tanner had the same view of women as Leather—that they needed big, strong men to protect them. "We used my barn hay and I was very, very careful not to hurt her, but she tossed me good once or twice. I was quick, but Anna was sure."

Tanner ran his hand through his waves, tilting his head in that old way, his eyes shadowed by those gleaming lashes, as though he was trying to understand. He lifted his head to scan the Smith ranch yard and fields, the house with its missing shingles and boards nailed over her bedroom window. His gaze lingered there, reminding her of how he'd tossed a pebble at her window years ago; he'd given her a wildflower bouquet at midnight and told her he loved her. Now the sound of his hand sliding slowly across his unshaven jaw caused her to shiver. "Invite me in, Gwyneth. Let's talk. I need answers."

"Is that why you came? To push and pry and ruin my life again?"

"You're hot-tempered too early in the morning—I wonder why? Is it because you know that I tried and you didn't? How many times did I try to talk with you? How many times did I call? And how many times did Leather lie for you, enjoying taunting me?" His finger strolled down her taut jaw. "I came to get my mother's two milk cows. You've got enough to do here without milking chores. But the yell sounded real interesting—I want answers, Gwyneth. Something is very wrong and it has been for years. You flinched when I touched you yesterday and again today. Haven't you gotten over that yet? Do I repulse you that much?"

For just a beat of her heart, Tanner's expression revealed that same quick shaft of confusion and pain. Then his look down at her was too mild, his half smile too practiced.

She swallowed, forcing moisture down her dry throat, for this man wasn't young Tanner; dark rivers of emotions ran through him now, and the mist seemed to pulse with his storms.

"Everything is just peachy. Go away." She wished she hadn't seen the doily escaping his jeans pocket. He missed Anna, and the painful task of separating her household possessions still awaited him and his sisters.

"Sure," he returned easily. "I knew you'd be too afraid to actually talk to me. Is that your studio, that addition onto the old house?"

He was a carpenter, learning from his father, a hand-craftsman and perfectionist. The addition she'd built was poor looking, but sturdy. She'd used old boards from a shack, read how to build a block foundation and set studs, but none of it could compare with the work Tanner could do. It was all hers, her safe place, where the potter's wheel hummed and fear and worry spun away in the clay. She couldn't let him into her life; she couldn't. "I've got work to do—"

"Sure you do, Gwyneth." His singsong taunt said he didn't believe her, that he knew she was trying to escape him. "You can yell now. I hear it's good therapy," he said before turning and strolling toward Anna's two milk cows.

Penny and Rolf followed at Tanner's heels. "Deserters," Gwyneth muttered darkly and tried not to notice how Tanner had become broader than the boy, his walk easy in the manner of a man who was proud, who knew who he was, and where he was going. As if he decided his fate. She resented that confidence, resented the hungry lingering of her gaze upon him. When Tanner reached to pet Sissy, she heard herself call, "You're no farm boy, Tanner Bennett, and those cows need milking twice a day. Make sure you let me know when you turn them back into my pasture, and make yourself scarce in the meantime. And don't you sell them to anyone but me. And don't you sell Anna's house until you let me—"

She hated swallowing the rest of the words. But the new well had cost too much and her mortgage to the bank wouldn't allow the purchase of Anna's home. Somehow she'd find a way, she always had, and she always paid her bills.

Tanner turned slowly, like a man who chose everything in his own time, not another's; he studied her across the small distance of the field. Then he blew her a kiss that sailed across the morning air and knocked her back into the old barn and pushed her breath from her body. "Don't you dare start up with me, Tanner Bennett," she heard herself whisper shakily. "Just go somewhere I'm not."

Late the next day, Tanner slapped his hand against the stack of new boards. Gwyneth drove herself too hard to keep the Smith ranch, doing enough work for two men. As a boy, Tanner had seen his mother too tired, pitting herself against work that was never done. He remembered the late nights when she made jams to sell, doing other people's laundry, and then sitting down with a pad and pencil and her checkbook to see what was left. She'd cleaned houses and baby-sat, and never once complained. As soon as he could, he helped, sending money home—there was college tuition for Kylie and Miranda, but Anna wanted nothing for herself; she was happy with what she had, with the balance in her life. Anna had achieved what most sought and couldn't find—peace.

But the frustration of seeing his mother work too hard, draining her body and mind to keep them together, to feed her growing family, had remained deep within Tanner. He'd been too young to help much, but he had, hiring out to ranchers for bailing, farm and cattle work. He'd hated the way his mother's shoulders drooped back then, weary from work, the way her hands were too broad and callused for a woman's, the way she'd made do with old clothes.

Now Gwyneth was doing the same thing, working too hard, trying to hold her land. Without looking at her hands, Tanner knew that Gwyneth's were callused and competent. The defined yet feminine muscles of her shoulders, arms and legs said she'd tested her strength to the limit. He'd planned to collect Anna's chickens, too, but Willa at the café had said that Gwyneth needed the egg-money, just like his mother had. He glanced at Koby Austin, who had come to help him build a new chicken house. Koby had lost a wife in childbirth and a son who never drew breath. Now his power saw tore across boards as fate had torn him apart. He glanced at Tanner and switched off the saw, lifting his safety glasses to his head. "This is like old times, isn't it? You and me working together, like when you came to help my folks build that barn. You were just twelve, when your dad died, and you hitched a ride to the ranch, toting your father's toolbox. My mother said you'd be a catch someday and that she was in love with you right then."

Tanner tossed Koby a cola from the small cooler. "My dad taught me a skill that will always serve me. Teaching wasn't for me and in the merchant marine, I made enough money to help Mom and my sisters. But I like the smell of new lumber, the feel of wood in my hands, waiting to come to life. I want this place in good shape—for Mom. I built the old chicken house when I was twelve and taking up where Dad had left off. It was my first project without him."

"Some say you'll sell, others say you Bennetts are like your mother, that Freedom Valley is where you'll settle. That means you'll be meeting Gwyneth upon occasion. Can you handle that? Or have you moved on since the last time you were moaning about how much you loved her?"

"Love can be evil and cold," Tanner said, tilting his cola high. "It's better to leave it behind."

They sat on the stack of new lumber, facing the Smith

ranch and sipped their colas in the shade of Anna's biggest oak tree.

Tanner took a long, assessing look at his friend and Koby smirked knowingly. "Nope. Never thought about asking Gwyneth out. Rejection isn't good for my psyche and besides that, it would seem incestuous, starting up with a good friend's woman. But if we're going to debate on the logic of women, we should do it in comfort—food, music and beer to ease the pain? In a righteous place where men come to understand the meaning of life and the intricacies of the female mind?"

Tanner lifted his eyebrow. "The Silver Dollar Tavern?"

Koby chugged the remainder of his cola and grinned. "I'll make a few calls. The Women's Council needs a little competition and we'll have our own meeting. Now that you're back, the rest of the pack will want in on this."

"Is the Women's Council still shoving men around?" Tanner remembered all that his mother had said about the ten women who had come from all parts of the world to settle in Freedom Valley. They'd banded together for protection, setting the rules for potential suitors who had to pass standards before marriage.

"You betcha. My sister, Rita, wouldn't have it any other way. She's a widow now, with kids and a small farm, and she's active in the Women's Council. My brothers, Adam and Laird, scoff at the tradition and Rita jumps them. Those ten women in the 1880s may have needed protection by sticking together, but Freedom Valley's women still have a fist hold on how a man treats a woman he wants. Our families are descended from those stubborn women who came to Montana and banded together, and times haven't changed much."

"So much for man's country. Did you court your wife according to the Rules for Bride Courting?"

"I did, and so did any man around here who wanted to stay on the good side of the Women's Council. You, my friend, did not. You rushed Gwyneth into marriage, and you've got a big red "Cull" marked on your backside. You may get a notice from the Women's Council to appear before them, just to set you straight. They really enjoy defining the rules of a Cull to someone who's been away. And you're prime for their picking. I'm not coming to the funeral."

Tanner took a long, deep breath filled with the scent of the newly mowed lawn. "Sometimes I wonder if things would have worked out—if I had followed the Rules for Bride Courting with Gwyneth... If I hadn't pushed her into marrying me so quickly."

Koby shrugged again, a man who had lost a wife and a baby. "You'll figure it out. Every man has to come to terms with the past and the here and now."

"You don't intend to marry again, do you?" Tanner asked his friend.

"Nope. I had a good marriage. I was happy. That's enough for me. It's more than some people have in a lifetime. Your mother was like that—happy with what she had. You still have a football we could toss around later, old man?"

Tanner sat brooding, dawn filtering through the lace curtains of his mother's quiet house. After the Bachelor Club's impromptu reunion at the Silver Dollar, he'd picked up a few bruises in the late-night football game. He couldn't sleep, his mind restless. He ran a finger over his mother's journals, neatly stacked on the polished dining room table that had been passed down from Magda

Claas, an ancestor on his mother's side. Beside Anna's journals was the prized English style teapot of a great-great grandmother on his father's side. Lined across the antique buffet were small framed pictures of the Bennetts and their ancestors.

Memories circled the rooms, his sisters' filled hope chests waiting upstairs in their rooms. Miranda and Kylie cared little for the tradition inherited from the Founding Mothers. His sisters had sprung into the outside world as he had done, only coming back to Freedom Valley to visit Anna. But his mother wanted them to have hope chests as she had had, and so for her, they embroidered hastily without really intending the use.

Young Gwyneth had fretted about her lack of a hope chest—old Leather hadn't allowed her to spend "silly time embroidering and such." Gwyneth had wanted to wait, to fill her hope chest as Tanner's sisters were doing—but there wasn't time and he'd pushed her....

Tanner ran his fingertip across the pineapple design of the table's doily, his mother's hook always flashing, a certain peace wrapped around her as she crocheted in the evenings, after the work was done. She'd learned from her mother and so on, the patterns handed down from Magda Claas. Kylie and Miranda never took time to learn, both of them too impatient.

He traced the frayed corners of the journals, letting his mother keep her secrets, her life, the thoughts that a woman would have at the end of the day. He'd seen her writing late at night, sometimes in bed. What gave her such strength to face raising her children, providing for them without a complaint?

Restless and unanswered questions prodding him, Tanner stood abruptly and scrubbed his hands across his unshaven jaw. Kylie and Miranda had promised to come back, to help sort their mother's things, but right now, Tanner needed answers to the past. He stretched out his fingers, missing the boats that he loved to build, the smooth wood sliding beneath his touch. He placed his open hand on one journal, wishing his mother were here, alive and smiling, baking bread...

Was it his right to read his mother's journals? Her private thoughts should remain her own and yet, he ached for his mother and wanted to hold her close.

He inhaled sharply and gently with one finger and the sense that he was prying, Tanner eased open one journal. He gently stroked the dried lavender stalk she'd pressed within the journal, the delicate fragrance wafting around him like memories. *My Life* his mother had written on the title page, the date just one year ago. "That night three years ago is stormy, just as my thoughts remain about the evil those men did to a sweet girl. I have never felt such anger in my life as when Gwyneth ran to me that night. The sight of her, torn and bleeding by those men's rough hands, just three days before she was to marry my son haunts me," she'd written in her precise, feminine hand. "I begged her to tell him before the wedding, and she couldn't bear to hurt Tanner. She talked to me of it, how she tried to push herself, and knew she should tell Tanner. Yet she couldn't. I kept my promise not to tell my son, but knew it was so wrong."

Tanner frowned and with a sense that his mother had reached out to him, to help him understand, sat down to read.

Three

Men have dark sides, deep brooding creatures that they are, filled with arrogance and swaggering when they are proud of themselves. But if a woman can capture a good man, she can tame him with the softness of her heart. Men go in packs sometimes to protect themselves from being captured. They're vulnerable creatures, needing petting and care, though they won't admit it. The boy within the man wants to play, while the man has headier thoughts that can make a woman's head spin.

—Anna Bennett

''Tanner Bennett, you are going to die,'' Gwyneth muttered as she peered out her kitchen window into the stormy dawn. In the half-light, Tanner's shaggy hair lifted in the wind and the powerful set of his broad shoulders stretched his T-shirt as he turned to set the plow's tines into the earth. As if in rage, his metal tractor-monster tore by her ancient one, which had sputtered and died before finishing the new garden.

An experienced man from the country, Tanner knew how to tear away and open earth as though he were laying siege to her land…and this time there was no Leather to stand between Tanner and her. ''I can deal with Tanner Bennett. And I will. I've dealt with everything else around here from mortgages to bad fences and dead tractors, and real-estate agents who wouldn't take 'no.'''

Gwyneth shook her head and ran her shaking fingers through her cropped hair, spiking it. One look in a mirror revealed her pale face and the circles beneath her eyes. All she needed after a draining night of bad dreams and hearing about last night's reunion of the Bachelor Club was Tanner outside her window. Here he was, starting up with her and she had work to do and deliveries to make. She glanced at the mugs she'd been carefully wrapping in newspaper and easing into a cardboard box to take to a tourist store in another town. The various shaped mugs, each stamped on the bottom with her trademark, provided a steady income, easy for tourists to pack and transport. Larger bowls, speckled in earth tones, were for Willa's Café, perfect for her soups. Gwyneth had built a steady clientele and by raising cattle and potting, she'd hauled herself out of all debt except the mortgage used to pay her father's medical expenses. And all without the help of an interfering ex-husband. She slapped her ball cap on her head, jerked on her battered denim jacket against the chilly April morning and glared at Penny and Rolf, who were whining to be let out. "You run to Tanner, grinning and drooling all over him, and you're going back to that cheap dog food for a week. And you're not going with me to make the deliveries today."

Undaunted by her threats, Penny and Rolf burst from the opened door, tails wagging on their way to Tanner.

She marched across the field, across a plowed strip and stood in front of his tractor, her hands on her hips. Wearing only a T-shirt against the morning chill, Tanner scowled at her, braked the tractor to a stop and clicked off the ignition. In one lithe jump, he was on the freshly plowed ground and tramping toward her. Gwyneth tried to ignore the angry shiver running through her and noted briefly that she'd never feared Tanner, except that night.

As he moved toward her, a tall powerful man she'd known all her life, his eyes flashing with anger, she shot at him, "You're in a fine mood. So you played football on the high school field after the Silver Dollar closed. My phone has been ringing steadily—as if I'm responsible for you. Well, I'm not. I heard all your old chums were there, married and unmarried boys alike, waking up half the town with yells and turning on their headlights. Look at you…you're bleary eyed, you're wearing a beard and you look like you'd like to tangle with a bear. Nelda Waters wasn't happy about Sam being invited to play at two o'clock in the morning, or about him having to drive their old tractor down to the high school ball field to sell to you. You could have waited until today. You're not young anymore, Tanner, and you've given the town enough gossip fodder. Your mother would have—"

"You've got a fast mouth on overdrive. You sound like someone's wife—but you're an *ex-wife,* aren't you?" He stood over her now, his grim expression sliding into a dark, wary, penetrating search of her face as though seeing beneath the surface. *"You should have told me."*

His words slashed through the cool morning air like a saber, pinning her, locking her boots to the spring earth. His determined, fierce expression told her that he'd set his mind to a task she didn't understand, but feared. She backed away until she stepped up on un-plowed ground, the sound of her heart pounding over the meadowlark's trill and the roosters' crowing. Tanner had come after her secrets, his eyes boring into her, and he looked as if nothing would move him until he had answers. She reached out her hand, anchoring her body, supporting her weak legs, and gripped her old tractor, a remembrance of Leather. But he wasn't here now, a protective wall between Tanner and herself. "Told you what?"

Tanner's glance seared her left hand, stripped of his wedding band. The grim lines between his brows and around his mouth deepened and anger flashed in his eyes. She'd never seen him as he was now, cold, powerful and deadly, not with the hot slap of temper, but enough cold determination to rip any hoarded secrets from her.

She had just one secret, other than their nonexistent wedding night, and he served it to her on a platter.

"That you were assaulted just three days before our wedding." The brutal statement sliced through her—no concessions, no tenderness. "You were on the interstate, stopped for gas, and when you got back in your car, they were waiting. Oh, they returned what was left of you all right, and went on their way, and you never told anyone but my mother. She put you together before you went back to Leather, because she knew what he'd do—either come after me with blood in his eye, suspecting me of doing it—or take a strap to you for enticing them. He wouldn't have believed what really happened...he wasn't the sort to believe that a woman wasn't to blame. No one else ever knew, *not even your husband.*''

Cold mist surrounded Gwyneth, taking away her breath, her nightmare flooding back through the dawn, tearing at her. Hands tearing at her, pushing her down— She tried to breathe, but couldn't. Her mouth opened and closed, but words wouldn't come. She struggled against the weight of the nightmare and the dark violence curling around Tanner now. ''There's only one way you could have gotten that information. You shouldn't have read your mother's journals. They were private.''

''I'm her son. She was ripped away too soon by that accident. I needed to...never mind. She's a part of me, just like she's a part of most everyone in the valley, especially you. I miss her. I wanted to hold onto her a bit longer. I read—damn, Gwyneth, you should have told me,'' he repeated, raking his hands through his hair.

She was too exposed, raw with pain now. She sucked breath into her lungs, her body damp with perspiration and so cold—

''That's the reason for guard dogs, for the locks and self-defense, and who knows what else, isn't it? That's the reason you ran,'' he stated bitterly. ''And not even old Leather knew a thing about the assault, did he?''

''I...'' She'd been ashamed, too hurt to tell anyone. A dark weight enclosed her, pushed her down and then Tanner was picking her limp body up and carrying her across the ranch yard into her house. In a dizzy whirl of mixed memories, she almost felt him carrying her body over the threshold of the motel that night.

He shouldered open the door, kicked it closed against

the dogs as though he didn't want any interference, and placed her in a kitchen chair. In brisk movements, Tanner poured hot water from the teakettle into her cup, slapped a tea bag in it, and turned to stare out the window, his hands on his hips, his body taut. He slammed his open hand onto the counter, the sound causing her to jerk. The boiling fury in his voice reached out to scorch her. "You knew that Leather wouldn't believe you, too, didn't you? So you didn't say anything—didn't report the men who went on their way, didn't tell Leather, and *you did not tell me.*"

Her cold hand couldn't feel the heat from the tea; her entire body would never be warm again. She hadn't wanted anyone to know and now—

He turned to her slowly, the shadows hiding the hard, bitter lines of his face. "My mother wanted you to tell me. She thought you would. But you didn't trust me enough. We were going to be married and—"

His fist hit the old scarred table and the mugs danced with the impact. Gwyneth dully watched them, the products of her new life threatened by the past. She heard the clatter and saw the ripples in her cup of tea and felt the blood leave her body. Her voice came through the distance, from a logical part of herself. "You would have tried to catch them. The whole countryside would have known what happened. I couldn't have faced that. Not then."

With a frustrated gesture, Tanner ran both hands through his shaggy hair. "Do you know what you've done to me, Gwyneth—sweet little Gwynnie? Do you know that I can't—that I look at a woman and remember your terror that night? How you looked at me, turned white and ran out the door? What do you think that does to a man?"

With a stark look of pain, he turned again from her. At his sides, his fists clenched tightly, the T-shirt stretched across the taut muscles of his back. The bitterness in his voice crackled about the sunlit room. "Drink your tea. You look half dead...someone should have tracked them down and—"

"I managed—" she heard herself say.

"The hell you did. One look at you says differently. You look like a ghost."

"I am a ghost," she said quietly, as a young, sweet Gwyneth waltzed happily across her mind.

Tanner impatiently reached for a kitchen tea towel and lifted her chin, carefully dabbing away the tears. Against her flesh, his fingers were hard and safe, trembling. Then, hurling the tea towel aside, he sat in an old chair and with a rough noise, scooped her upon his lap, pushing her head against the safe, warm cove of his shoulder and throat. She knew she should stand free, to be strong, but just then, the nightmare enveloped her, choking her, she couldn't leave his warm, strong arms. Tanner pressed his face next to her hair and his hard body trembled around her, his hands opened and gathered her protectively against him. "You should have told someone, Gwyneth. Those men should have paid," he whispered shakily and began to rock her.

"I just couldn't. They weren't from here—just two strangers passing through on the interstate. It was dark and I couldn't identify them, even if I'd wanted to press charges." She hadn't been held like this for years, since before that night, and then the thought of a man holding her too close terrified her. It devoured her and she tore from him, gripping the kitchen counter and breathing hard, pushing air into her lungs, trying to force the nightmare away. "You should go now," she managed to say.

"It isn't just me, is it? It's any man who comes close to you?" he asked quietly, watching her.

This time, she grabbed the tea towel and swiped it roughly across her damp face. "Please, Tanner. Just go."

"You're killing yourself here, trying to make it on your own, just like my mother, and I'm a part of it all. Do you think I can forget that night any more than you can? How it was, so sweet and beautiful with all of our dreams spread before us—and then, suddenly everything was gone." Tanner pushed himself to his feet. "We're not done yet, sweet Gwyneth mine—Mrs. Bennett," he said, before slamming the door behind him.

Okay, he was a brute, Tanner decided six weeks later. He stood aside in late May's sunshine as Brody Thor's truck poured concrete into the foundation of the new building. Brody was the town's "bad boy" spawned by a drunken father and a woman who left town as soon as she could. After a few minor scrapes with the law, and a lifetime of meals at Anna's well-stocked table, Brody had married at seventeen. When his young wife left him for a better prospect, he raised his two daughters, worked hard and fitted seamlessly into life in Freedom Valley. And Anna had helped.

Gabriel Deerhorn and Dylan Spotted Horse, lifetime friends of Tanner, stood waiting as the gray mix plopped into the area they had prepared. "So you decided to stay a bit," Brody said, drawing on his leather gloves. He scanned the wooden form Tanner had built to shape the concrete floor. "You'd know how to do this. Your dad built half the houses in Freedom Valley and most of the barns."

"Valentinia Lake has plenty of fishing, so do the other

lakes around. And there's always the buyer who will
travel a bit for a handmade boat.'' Tanner bent to smooth
the concrete with Gabriel and Dylan. A fast trip to the
coast, to sell his business to a waiting buyer, and to
collect his tools, had given him thinking room. But the
image of Gwyneth huddled over that kitchen table, her
shoulders bent as though taking a blow, had haunted
him.

She hadn't trusted him.

The men who violated her would never be caught;
she'd never have closure. He frowned at the gray cement
beneath his trowel, noting that in his anger, he'd created
a groove. He resmoothed the surface and moved on to
the next blob of concrete that Brody had just poured.

*Whatever else he did in his life, he had to finish that
night when Gwyneth's eyes had widened at his bare
chest, when she'd flown from their marriage.... He had
to untangle the past, give them both peace. And she was
killing herself with hard work, the same as his mother.*

A low wolf whistle and Brody's nod took Tanner's
eyes to the country road and a sleek, black Mercedes
prowling alongside Gwyneth and her dogs. ''That would
be Noah Douglas. Came back to the valley to run an
investment service. She started that running a few days
after you left. Noah makes it a point every so many days
to drive down that road just about the time she's jogging.
Maybe he likes the hot-looking, sweaty woman type.''

''Noah may dress in a pin-striped suit, but he's still
country,'' Gabriel noted. ''He's a good man. Then
there's John Lachlan at the bank, who would like to help
Gwyneth with her mortgage. She's not having any per-
sonal attention, though, from anyone.''

Gabriel grinned as Tanner shot a dark look at him.
''That is a very particular woman. Those dogs don't let

too many men near her. She keeps to herself, or she's busy with the Women's Council. I saw her waltz into the Silver Dollar Tavern one night and take Lundy Vincent, twice her size, apart. Before I could stop the argument and protect her, she started with Lundy. She went after him for hurting his wife. He took offense to her shaking her finger beneath his nose and reached for her. He ended up on the floor with her boot on his throat and the promise on his lips that he'd leave Sue alone. There was something else riding Gwyneth that night. I've never seen her so mad. I'd call it rage. I think she frightened herself...she was shaking and white. She wasn't frightened when she took him down. She looked like the men clapping for her were next on her list.''

Tanner narrowed his eyes as he stood, tracing the woman flying down the road, long legs flashing and the damp T-shirt pasted to her gently bobbing breasts. He knew what was riding Gwyneth, the pain and humiliation she had suffered. In the dappled light of the trees along the road, her skin gleamed over slender, defined muscles. She looked so free and strong, the dogs racing at her side.

Yet neither one of them were free, trapped by fate.

At sunset, Tanner knocked on her door, smiling briefly as Penny and Rolf rushed at him, tails wagging, for their treats. He tucked the fragrant plants, wrapped in wet newspaper and a plastic sack, beneath his arm and tossed the doggy cookies to the dogs, then circled the house. In the addition built of old boards and framed by poorly fitted windows, he saw Gwyneth. She bent over her potter's wheel, her hands gracefully shaping a bowl, the dying light skimming her fair hair. Clay splattered her T-shirt and her bare arms and legs, her expression intent upon her work. Made of old planks, the shelves held mugs and bowls newly "thrown" and set to dry, and colorful jars of glazes.

Tanner pushed open the door to speak her name and then she turned to him—her expression still soft and brooding, intent upon her work. As she looked at him in the doorway, the untended, whirling wet bowl slowly collapsed. Her hands, slick with potter's clay, stayed above the wheel, her mouth parted in surprise.

"I have to know, Gwyneth," he whispered softly above the whirring of the wheel. "If I'd have courted you by the valley's customs, if you had trusted me more. If I had given you more time to adjust to the idea of marriage, maybe you could have told me, eventually, what happened to you. I would have understood then—"

"It's done. We're done." Above the circling wheel and the failed bowl, her hands clenched into fists and then her eyes closed. She reached to dip her hands in the bucket at her side and briskly wipe them with an old rag before turning off the electric-powered wheel. She stood in the shadows of the roughly crafted studio, clay splattered across her face. "Why did you come back? What are you building at Anna's? When are you leaving?" she shot at him bitterly.

Tanner tried to force away the leap of anger and failed. He crushed the plant starts in his fist. She'd torn away his life—hers had been destroyed and there had to be an end. "If I had courted you, would it have made a difference?" he pushed at her again. "Would you have trusted me then?"

"Stop. Just stop. What's done is done," she answered tightly, her face pale beneath the drops of clay.

"It isn't done and you know it." He almost smiled for it was her anger, not her fear, leaping now. He sensed it filling the small quiet studio, trembling hotly around the drying pots and quivering in the delicate ferns.

Then Gwyneth bent, scooped up the ruined pot with her fists and hurled it at him.

The clay hit him and so did his temper. Tanner slapped the plastic sack filled with plants into her hands, picked her up and carried her outside into the dying light. He dumped her in an old bathtub, which served to water the stock. "Cool off, Gwynnie."

She bobbed up, hands braced to lift herself free and in that instant, the damp cloth pasted to her breasts revealed the dark peaks of her nipples. The sensual jolt hit Tanner in his midsection, his body hardening.

Then because he wanted to hold her and keep her safe and couldn't stop the dangerous storm of emotions between them, Tanner reached down, cupped the back of her head, kissed her hard and damned himself for the sweet need that hadn't died in years.

He hadn't expected her arms circling his neck, crushing the fragrant herbs between them. The hot, sweet hungry promise of her mouth burned him and Tanner found himself unbalanced. Falling, taking care not to crush her, Tanner twisted to plop into the other end of the tub. He caught her ankles, preventing her escape, and with the cold water sloshing around them as a cow came to drink, the dogs to nuzzle her hands for reassurance, Gwyneth glared at him.

Still shocked that she had reached for him, kissed him, he couldn't help but laugh at the fierce scowl, droplets of clay clinging to her hair and face. Was that sunlight, or was it happiness curling around him? How long had it been since he'd laughed so freely?

"Why did you come?" she asked furiously between

her clenched teeth as he noted the neat fit of her bare, delicate feet within his large hands.

Because she was bracing to run away and he wanted more of this Gwyneth, the angry, frustrated and hungry one, he glanced at her breasts, the dark nipples peaking the damp cloth. "My, my, my. What would the Women's Council say about that?"

She glanced down, shot a scowl at him and grabbed the plastic sack of plants floating in the water between them. Using lavender, oregano, fennel and thyme as shields, she crossed her arms over her chest and slid down into the water. "That was evil. This water is cold. Look the other way while I get out."

"Nope," he drawled and couldn't help the grin that followed as free as the lavender bloom floating toward him. He blew it back toward her.

Pleased that Gwyneth had shocked herself, had reached for him and thrust her lips against his, Tanner studied the stunning mix of emotions racing across her face. She hadn't planned to touch him; she hadn't planned to *need*. For just that heartbeat, her walls had been tossed aside. She was uncertain now, of herself and of him. But whatever she was feeling, it wasn't the fear that had ruined their lives. He drew the lavender beneath his nose, inhaling the fragrance that brought his mother to mind.

"I am sorry, Gwyneth," he said simply, meaning it and watching the soft tremble of her mouth. He was sorry for so many things, for rushing her, for taking what he wanted, for not giving her enough time to trust him.

She turned to him, waves of anger pouring off her. "Don't you dare feel sorry for me. I've managed. Anna was my friend. I loved polishing furniture that meant so much to her. Others helped."

"You're working yourself too hard here, Gwyneth—" He'd seen another woman struggle against hardships and the bitterness rose within him.

"You have nothing to say about that. Let go of my feet, Tanner, or I'll set the dogs on you."

"Do that, why don't you? Set your guard dogs on me?" he asked as Penny and Rolf angled to lick his face and whined for an ear-scratching. He ran his thumbs over the arches of Gwyneth's slender feet, enjoying the play of soft flesh and bones within his hands, as she glared furiously at him. He reveled in the excitement rushing through him, the heady sense that he'd come home, found what he'd searched for—or had he?

With a sense that everything was coming full circle, Tanner stood up and stepped from the tub. He bent to lift Gwyneth and place her on her feet. Her arms remained crossed on her chest, the plants drooping over her arms, her glare burning him. Tanner ripped off his wet T-shirt and hurled it back into the water, needing to know how she would respond to the sight of him, his body no longer sleek as a boy, but hard and corded and lightly furred at his chest. There had been just that frustrated lick of hunger when she'd kissed him, enough to soothe the ego she'd dented years ago.

He studied the widening of her eyes as she traced his muscular arms and shoulders, lingering on the droplets upon the black hair of his chest. The dainty flick of her tongue and the hot color of her cheeks said that she hadn't forgotten the hunger that ran between them all those years ago, when he'd wanted to wait for his wedding night and his virgin bride.

"I would have understood," he said quietly, aching for her. "I would have waited until you were ready, until you wanted me."

She looked down at her bare feet, toes curled in the new grass, shivering with uncertainty now, not the cold water. "I wasn't the same. They say men know these things."

"I would have understood," he repeated, wishing he could hold her close. "You've been thinking about me, haven't you? Wondering how it would have felt—"

"I know how it feels. I'd seen farm animals rut and that's just how it was, only I was fighting, and then I went into myself," she interrupted bitterly, reminding him that her body had been torn carelessly, hurriedly.

At least she was talking to him, Tanner thought, after he recovered from the brutal image. He had to keep her talking, to keep that contact. *Come on, Gwyneth. You've held this in for years…let go…stay here with me…don't close me away.* "When people care, it isn't like that, and we cared. Remember how it was between us, how sweet it was to lie in the grass and kiss and hunger and touch—the hot, sweet need making you purr beneath me and plan the babies we would make when the time was right…."

Her eyes widened. "I never touched you like that."

"No, we were both careful, because we wanted marriage. You sent me home many a night with an ache—I remember the heady scent of you, coming through your clothes, the way you breathed unevenly against my skin and when I touched you—"

Gwyneth stiffened, her fingers digging into her upper arms. "You never touched me. You never put your hands anywhere they weren't supposed to be."

"But I wanted to, and you did, too, your hips lifting to mine. That's how lovemaking is supposed to be—warm, intimate, gentle, like the sliding of your fingers between mine, our palms together, a cherishing shared between us. At times, it should be like rolling on an ocean wave, warm and soft and sweet.'' He knew she couldn't understand the lovemaking—the tempest, the driving hunger, bodies thrusting to seek the ultimate release.

But he wanted more with Gwyneth. To deny that, his heart and soul would label him a liar.

Her mouth had parted at the picture and she blinked, crushing the bundled herbs in her arms. ''How you talk, Tanner Bennett. Is that how you—?''

He knew her question, shamed that he'd taken women for momentary needs, his and theirs. He was a man who needed more than sex to fill him. Because of her innocence of the world, he wanted to let her know— ''I've had women.''

She stared at him curiously and the lavender stalk clung to her cheek unnoticed. ''Did you get all hot and shaky like when you were younger? When you put me away from you and wouldn't kiss me anymore? Were they one-night stands, or—''

''Lay off.'' He was both pleased that she was interested, and nettled by her innocence to his jaded experience. His ''experience'' was limited, because she'd always been there when he'd touched another woman. He was hot and shaking with Gwyneth because he'd been leashing the need to have her, keeping her righteously safe until their wedding night. So much for righteous intentions.

She tilted her head, peering at him curiously. ''When was the last time? I mean, I've heard that men can't go long without—''

''It's been a while,'' he returned tightly, getting uncomfortable now.

"Well, I mean, just what does it take to get you interested…aroused?" she persisted.

"Women who do not wear bras," he answered grimly to slow her questions and put her off; he damned Leather for not explaining more to his daughter.

"Karolina doesn't always wear bras. She says they ruin the line of some outfits and that some women wear pointy ones and some wear soft ones because of what men like. Why did you just groan and close your eyes?"

Tanner shook his head, clearing it of the image of Gwyneth's damp breasts. "Gwynnie, let's just leave it for now, okay? I'm not your brother or your father. I'm an ex-husband. There's a big difference."

She blinked again, those hazel eyes gathering up the lush green of the plants in her arms. "Just talking about women's underwear gets you bothered?"

"If you'll remember, I never got yours off. That was a considerable mistake that haunts me." He resented the surly darkness of his tone and her prying into his desire.

"You never tried. You were always so sweet."

He wasn't feeling sweet now, but Gwyneth's voice was indignant as though she were protecting him. No one had protected him in a very long time. He ran a finger across the clay on her nose, unable to resist the tease. "Mother would have wanted you to have those herb starts, an inheritance of sorts from a woman who loved you," he said, nodding at the sad and dripping plants in her hands, the plastic sack filled with water. His sisters had promised to come, to retrieve what they wanted, and they'd surely give Gwyneth more.

Dealing with a woman who was more innocent than she knew wasn't easy when a hunger ran through him to hold her close and kiss those parted, shocked lips. "In answer to your question of what am I doing, I'm setting up my boat business and I'm settling into Freedom Valley. Ah, it's a grand life, Gwyneth Smith Bennett, and it's a fact that you did kiss me. You'll have to come for me if you're wanting more kisses, because this time, I'm not pushing. You set your own time to come calling,'' he couldn't resist adding, reminding her of when she took his name, that sweet time long ago.

She tramped around Anna's two-story house, careful of the mid-June's new irises and yellow tulips, calling him out. She'd managed to avoid Tanner for two weeks while he and his friends worked on the big wooden building behind Anna's. Men could do amazing things when they wanted to, and if she'd had any help like that, she could have—

"Things come easy to some, and to others they don't.'' The day she'd thrown a ruined pot at him, he'd caught part of her, softened a bleak memory with another.

She couldn't forgive him for listening, for knowing too much—and for having her dog. When he didn't answer her knock on Anna's back door, she tramped past the sleek black monster of a pickup. She marched through the yawning open doors of his new building. The scented bite of paint and varnish, softened by new lumber, met her. Over the doors, a neatly blocked sign proclaimed the name of his new business, The Boat Shop. The open windows lining both sides of the barn-like structure let in the June sun. In one corner stood a drafting board with a sketch pinned to it, more sketches tacked along the wall, and the clutter of an office rambled around it. In the center of the space were wooden sawhorses, and amid a row of overhead lights, a heavy-duty hoist waited to be lowered.

She recognized the big oak rocking chair that had been his father's, solidly made for a man of height and weight. As children, Miranda and Kylie had sat squeezed into the chair with their dolls, making room for her. Anna's voice had softened when she spoke of Tanner rocking his new baby sisters in just that chair. "He'll make a fine family man," Anna had said softly. "Just like his father. A woman couldn't want for more. He'll find his love and he'll never wander. His heart is true and good and kind. He'll care for her all the days of his life and she'll never want for love."

The wood gleamed now, the broken arm repaired and sturdy. Two smaller rocking chairs, more ornate and meant for lighter weight had been stripped of coatings, waiting for new. Heavy wood clamps held tight a thick wooden claw foot from Anna's four-poster bed. Shelved lumber lined the walls and from a rooftop skylight, the sunlight outlined Tanner, bent over his work.

Dressed in a black T-shirt, cutoff denim shorts and canvas shoes, he concentrated on the board he was smoothing at his workbench. He ran his hand over the wood in a caress. Sawdust caught the midmorning light, swirling around him, the muscles of his arms shifting beneath tanned skin as he worked, his body flowing into his work. He glanced up, noted her standing in the huge doorway, and continued to work, a Celtic flute playing softly amid the shadows, circling him. When he turned to her, an earring hoop gleamed in his ear, nestling amid the shaggy cut of his hair.

Caught by his exotic look, the hard rhythmic shift of muscles beneath his clothing, a hard muscle on his backside tightening and running down his legs, his big hands flowing over the wood, Gwyneth fought for breath, her

stomach clenching. Tanner was beautiful amid his work,
the rhythm of his body almost sensual—

She found Penny suddenly at her side, nuzzling her
hand, and at Rolf's whine, she scanned the shadows. He
attempted to rise, a white bandage circling his middle
and one back leg. He whined again, as defeated, he lowered to the old quilt folded beneath him. She hurried to
him, kneeled by his side, crooned to him and stroked his
ears until he settled, Penny at his side. The bandages and
scrape marks over Rolf's body said he was lucky to survive. She held his head and soothed him and tried not
to cry.

The shadows stirred behind her and Tanner said,
"He's doing fine."

Gwyneth forced herself to her feet, glaring at him.
"You should have contacted me."

"I tried. You're a busy woman. It seems that the
Women's Council Sweetheart Dance and Ice-Cream Social is taking a lot of your time. Rolf is badly bruised,
scraped and sedated, and he's not going anywhere right
now."

"You can't keep my dog." She didn't want to owe
Tanner anything. She didn't want her life to blend with
his.

"The vet doesn't want him moved for a couple of
days. I'll take good care of him. And, Penny. You're
welcome to visit anytime."

When Tanner sauntered to his corner office space and
sprawled upon a chair, bracing his canvas shoes upon a
cluttered, battered desk of sawhorses and planks, Gwyneth slapped her bare thigh, anger simmering. She continued slapping it all the way to him and stood while he
leisurely poured coffee from a thermos. "How dare you
take Rolf to the vet," she forced herself to say quietly

when she wanted to rip an oar from the wall and—
"He's my dog."

"He had to have care and quick. We'll probably never
know what happened to him, but he's been hit by a car
or truck. He crawled this far—and I took him to the
vet." Tanner sipped the coffee, then placed his arms
behind his head and leaned back, studying her. "You
thought you could make it work, didn't you? You
thought you could ignore what happened to you. No
wonder you were so white and shaking that night."

Waves of the past washed over her, slamming into her
with enough force to take away her breath. She forced
herself back to her mission, back from the torn dreams
and pain. Tanner was working through her nightmare in
his meticulous, determined way. If she wasn't careful,
he'd have more of her than she wanted to give. "You
shouldn't have paid the vet bill. He's taken payments
from me before."

She dug into her pockets and flung bills upon his desk.
The money was to have gone for a new well pump, the
old one barely alive. "I won't be owing you, Tanner
Bennett."

"You're in a fine froth," he said, using words inherited from his mother. He stared darkly at the crushed
bills, quickly grabbed from her cookie jar, as if he saw
them for what they were—her pitiful savings. Then he
turned slowly to her, the shadowy light laying upon the
hard planes of his jaw, the muscle shifting rhythmically
beneath tanned skin. "I should have known there was
something else. You are afraid to live, Mrs. Bennett.
You're afraid to touch and feel and listen to the music
in your heart. You're afraid of me, except when that
high-wide temper is ruling you."

"I'm not afraid of anything."

"You're afraid to talk with me. You're afraid to ask me to the dance." His taunt curled softly, deadly around her, twining around her heart and squeezing it.

"This won't work," she whispered shakily as Tanner came lithely to his feet, towering over her. "Ask you to the dance?" she repeated, stunned. "You know that the Sweetheart Dance is a kickoff for any men that want to court brides, and that the women do the asking to it. Married couples and singles enjoy it, but it's one of the Rules for Bride Courting when a woman asks a man to the dance. I usually don't dance anyway...I work the concessions and clean and—" She seldom danced, for that meant to be held in the arms of a man, and she couldn't bear that.

He reached out his hand toward hers, and instinctively she jerked back. Tanner's soft smile was sad and knowing as he picked up the ringing telephone near her hand. "The Boat Shop...that's right, handmade, one- to two-man fishing boats, sit low in the water with custom-made oars, all wood lapstrake—overlapped wood."

While studying her, he quoted the potential customer a range of prices that took her breath. When he was finished, Gwyneth was stunned. "People pay that much?"

Tanner shrugged. "Handmade, good work meant to last. I owe my friends each one for helping me day and night on this building. They'll come in to help with their own boats. By fall, we'll have a fishing tournament. Brody is building his girls a pair of 'wee lassie' canoes in the back—small, light and built for one. He's putty in their hands and it was the name, 'wee lassie,' that sold him, not the design. You might tell the Women's Council that they are welcome to build their own, with my help. If they don't want sea kayaks or skiffs, maybe a smaller pram or dory would do.''

"You did all this, just like that? Learned a skill so removed from the valley?''

He tilted his head to one side, studying her. "So what potter did you learn from here in the valley?''

"I learned from library books and by going to craft shows and talking to people. Because of his hands, an older man had to quit the craft. I bought his old gas kiln and assembled it here. He gave me a few lessons to start me off. It was wonderful—'' She shrugged, hoping her greed for a new kiln and wheel wouldn't show. She was making a tidy living from her time spent at the wheel in mugs and bowls. "I haven't worked up to lamps yet and some of my lids don't always fit the pots. When I move up to lamps and canisters and tureens, I'll be making more money.''

She could work a lifetime and never have enough to buy one boat. She ran her hand across her forehead, a headache lurking behind her brows. Tanner didn't have to leave Freedom to work...he'd brought his business with him. She studied the sketch on his drafting board, the lettering and measurements in Tanner's neat blocky style. "That's the plans for a boat?''

Tanner nodded toward the framed pictures on the wall, some of them mirroring the brilliant June sunlight. Men in the low-riding boats held up fish for the camera. "I'd like to set up a sawmill in a year or so.''

"A year or so," she repeated dully, her hopes that Tanner would leave soon shredding onto the concrete floor at her boots.

A shaft of sunlight careened off the picture glass and hit Tanner's frown. "Lydia Mae Collins informed me that Culls weren't welcome at the dance, not unless an unmarried woman invites them. The only reason I'm a Cull is because of you, sweetheart, because I was too anxious to make you my wife and take you with me. That was a mistake. I didn't know you wouldn't trust me, confide in me how you'd been hurt... Are you going to ask me to the dance or not?'' Bitterness lay in his deep, easy tone, and she felt the lick of it skittering up her bare arms.

"People would talk," she answered, wishing for her safe life without the complications of Tanner, who bore the scent of fresh wood and man. He knew as well as she that in Freedom, people repaid favors, and he'd probably saved Rolf's life by acting quickly. She'd find some way to repay him, other than— "Can't someone else ask you to go?"

Tanner slid his hands into his back pocket. "I've had a nibble or two, but I'm choosy. It seems only fitting that the woman who cost me my dating rights in Freedom Valley might serve them back up to me."

She snorted at that. "'A nibble.' You've had more women over here, bringing you pies and casseroles, and I heard about every one of them. They're ready to throw away sense and the Rules for Bride Courting just to get you, like a big trophy. One or two of them thought I wouldn't mind sharing tips on how to handle you—since we haven't been an item for years, they thought I might want to pass you on to them."

His smile wasn't nice, nor his low drawl that raised the hairs on her nape and pinned her wildly racing heart within her breast. He placed a finger beneath her chin and gently lifted, closing her parted lips. "But not you, Gwyneth. You haven't been nibbling."

Then she knew: Tanner wanted revenge for the humiliation of having been a bridegroom left on his wedding night, and he would have it in front of the whole town. He wasn't a man to be easily put off and she was in for a fight.

Four

A man needs to be needed and to be shown in front of others that he is the one choice of the woman he loves. That is why it is the custom in Freedom Valley for a woman to ask the man for the last dance. This will be no easy task for my son, because he is old-fashioned and proud and is likely to be going after the woman he wants, regardless of safety, as he follows his heart.

—Anna Bennett

Tanner studied the rain slashing at the windows, the mid-June storm whipping through the tree limbs beside the house. At three o'clock in the morning, he wished for the sea rolling beneath his feet, pitting himself against the punishing dark waves. Lightning forked down from the sky, and the stark outline of trees bent by wind leaped before him. His mother's lavender bed, and all the rest, herbs he'd never taken time to know, were flattened by the beating rain.

He'd loved her, cherished her, but he didn't know her. He didn't know her strength and what gave her peace—he didn't understand...

She had liked her life plain, she'd said, giving him a kiss and a hug to soften his bruised pride when he'd offered to help. But her hand gently stroking his cheek had shaken him more than her tender words, "You must make peace with Gwyneth, too, for there are things she can't tell you. When the time is right, you'll know. Search your heart then, and see if you wouldn't have done the same."

He frowned, temper ruling him when he thought of Gwyneth roughly handled, their lives torn apart. His fists wanted to hit something, someone, to make them pay. How many times had he tried to patch himself together, tried to shift his dreams onto another woman, another face and body. Understanding Gwyneth's trauma didn't salve his dark mood, the time lost in their lives, and the way she was working too hard.

He'd rather battle the storm at sea than face his emotions about his ex-wife.

Lightning speared the black sky and he saw the hunched shadow battle open the door of his workshop and slide within. "I knew she'd come—"

Careful not to hurt Rolf, Gwyneth shivered, snuggling down into her sleeping bag, her hands upon Rolf's and Penny's heads. "I missed you."

She sighed, safe now, curled amid her warm dogs, the storm slashing outside the building, lighting the room with each flash of lightning, the thunder roaring outside like a dragon that wanted feeding.

The door tore open, letting in a gust of cold rain and outlining the taut, bold figure of a man, standing still to allow his eyes to adjust to the dim light. "There you are," Tanner said too softly, closing the door.

Before she could struggle free of the sleeping bag, to gather excuses around her, Tanner kneeled at her side, zipping the bag higher to imprison her. The flat of his hand against her chest pushed her down. Rain dripped from his face, plastering his hair on his head. An impatient toss of his head sent the strands flying out, hitting her face with a light spray of water. With a dark shadow cruising over his jaw, and the stark lightning harshly outlining the rain-wet planes of his face, Tanner resembled a warlord set upon revenge. "So here you are. Came for another kiss, did you?"

"You're in an evil mood, and you know I came to check on Rolf and Penny."

"They're fine. I've been here with them all night, except to check on my mother's house. Rolf shouldn't be moved. Now tell me why you're shivering and why you're out on a night like this."

The rap of his words reminded her of her bullying father; that male arrogance would not again make her feel as if she were owned and made to be ruled. She didn't want to tell Tanner anything, to let him into her life. He'd already stepped inside and knew too much. She damned the steady sneezing that left her gasping for breath. Three hours of herding frightened cattle back into the fallen fences without her dogs had left her icy cold and exhausted. Another hour of makeshift mending fences had taken the last of her and the cold house waited. Too exhausted to do more, she simply closed her eyes against Tanner's dark, angry expression. "I hope you're milking the cows regularly. They'll hurt if you don't," was all she could manage before more sneezing took her.

His hand was big and cool and rough on her forehead, the slightly rough back testing her cheeks for warmth. "You're burning up. I'm taking you to the doctor."

She fought the chill in her bones, gathering the battered sleeping bag around her. "No, I can't afford doctor bills or medicine. Just let me sleep—"

Tanner scooped her up, sleeping bag and all and carried her to the door. "Keep your head down," he ordered, tucking her close against him as he ran into Anna's house.

Freezing, shivering and hating her weakness, Gwyneth felt herself placed on a sofa, Anna's familiar living room curling around her. Running his hands through his hair, Tanner tore away his damp T-shirt and looked down at her. "You need a hot shower, plenty of hot tea and a good night's sleep from the shadows under your eyes. What's it going to be, Gwyneth? Me or the doctor? Can you stand to have me help you, or do I call—?"

She couldn't afford more bills; the cookie-jar money was all she had. Lightning outside lit his powerful chest and shoulders and she closed her eyes against the sight, too raw and masculine to give her peace. "A cup of tea would be nice and then I'll be on my way," she managed to whisper through her sore throat.

"So proper," he mocked her. "You need more than a cup of tea, and you need it now." He reached his hand for the zipper of her sleeping bag and held it still, waiting for her to agree. When she reluctantly nodded, Tanner eased away the sleeping bag.

"Stop cursing," she muttered, too hot now and fearing a fever that would cost her days of work. "I was only chasing cattle. My bull tore through a patch of fence, and took the posts with him. When it storms, cattle start up. It's a part of ranching, of country life."

"That's what my mother used to say. You're soaked clear through," Tanner said, scowling at her, and yet he waited.

"Why don't you go back to your sea?" she muttered and when he didn't answer, she shook her head, accepting what must be. Gwyneth knew her alternatives and Tanner would know what to do, he'd seen his mother work on fevers: If she got too sick, she'd lose work time and there would be medical bills she couldn't pay. "Do it," she said and closed her eyes, fighting the fear of a man's hands touching her. "Just do it."

"You sound like a virgin sacrifice to the volcano gods," he muttered darkly and propped her into sitting position. He eased her wet jacket from her and tugged away the sleeping bag. He went to work on her cold feet, discarding her thick, wet socks. He picked her up and carried her into the bathroom by the kitchen, turned on the shower and through the rising steam, looked down at her. "It works better without your clothes."

She fumbled for her buttons and knew he wanted to help, hovering over her. "I can manage."

His solid curse, one she'd never heard, trimmed in salt and sea, boiled through the steamy room. "'You can manage.' You're half dead, pitting yourself against that run-down ranch—"

She blew away the clinging drop on the end of her nose and wished she could blow him away as easily. "You're pushing me and I don't like that. I've had enough of pushy men in my life, and that includes you deciding that we had to get married right then, right away.''

That bit of brutal truth shocked him, the bitter resentment of a woman slapping at him. The girl had been helpless to express herself, but the woman came out with well-placed barbs, likening him to a known bully.

''I made a mistake. I know that now,'' he said after a pause in which the shower sounded like thunder between them.

She swatted his chest with her open hand, angry with him and with herself. ''Oh, you know I worshiped you then. The swaggering football hero who could charm any woman he wanted, and you chose me—plain, shy, quiet me. Older and with a smile that took any woman's breath away, you set your sights on me. You had this quiet way of talking, of just holding my hand, like I gave you something you needed. I wanted to be important to you, to please you. Maybe it was my fault, too, maybe I was looking for a way to leave Leather—he was a hard man. But things have changed, Tanner. It's my land and it's my life. I know how you hated the hard work your mother did, how you wanted better for her. But she liked work and so do I.''

He pushed his fingers through his damp waving hair, his expression frustrated. ''You're all eyes, and you look like you could use a good meal.''

Her chin went up with that. ''There's nothing wrong with the way I eat.''

His scowl lowered to hers, then his black gaze ripped down the towel she held protectively between them, though she still wore clothing. ''You've got curves, but you're lean and hard and your hands—''

He jerked her hand up, revealing the callused palm, the scratches from the brambles clinging to the fallen fence. His silence condemned and the muscle in his jaw clenched before he flung her hand away. With a last glare, he stepped outside the bathroom, causing the steamy mist to swirl behind him. The door clicked with a cold finality that tore at her. She shakily reached out her hand to turn the old lock and click it, earning safety for a few moments from Tanner's grim mood.

In the stream of hot water, Gwyneth shivered, her teeth chattering. She'd seen anger, disgust and concern in Tanner's expression. How long had it been since anyone had worried about her—except Anna?

Did she disgust him then, a man who knew what a woman's body should be, how it should feel to make love, the caring kind? She braced the flat of her hands against the tile, letting the shower warm her cold flesh, forcing herself to do the job, just as she always had. When she was young, Leather said he didn't have time nor money for sickness, and he'd taught her the rawhide-rough way of caring for herself. Gradually the hot water seeped through to her bones, and in her way, gained by practice, she pulled herself together, trying to push words and phrases into a defense against Tanner.

Then the shower curtain ripped open again, and she sheltered her naked body with her arms and hands.

"You've been in here too long," Tanner said. He studied her face, the water sluicing between them like memories. She could have shared her life with him—but that time was gone now and a hard man stood in the boy's place. Tanner was bitter now—after that night, he'd come to see her and Leather had knocked him to the ground. She'd flung herself over him, protecting him, and then had torn herself away, running into the house. She'd taken his pride and left him bitter. "I'm okay."

His black eyes sliced down her body, then up to her

face. "Tea is ready. Put Mother's herbal salve on your chest before you come out, and some ointment on those hands," he said before the shower curtain ripped closed again.

Tanner cursed again later, when she slid into the kitchen chair, her hair wet and combed by her fingers, her body dressed in his overlarge sweat clothes, hung by the door. "I've got to be going."

"The hell you will. You're staying until I know that you don't have pneumonia. What were you thinking of—going out on a night like this without rain gear? Those cattle could have been rounded up in the morning," he shot at her. "Drink that tea."

"People will talk," she grumbled.

"They've talked about us before. I'll be here this time to face them with you."

"It will be worse than before. I'm on the Women's Council. I can't be staying overnight with an unmarried man and no one else in the house."

"Oh, yes. How would that look? A night with your ex-husband, the one you didn't bed," he said darkly, as if circling a battle he intended to win. He grabbed a towel from the back of the chair, slapped it none too gently over her head and rubbed with the same carelessness, as though he couldn't bear to touch her. "Drink."

The tangy scent told her that he hadn't forgotten his mother's blend of lemon and peppermint and honey. She sat still, knowing better than to move, when he returned with a hair dryer and began using it on her hair, his big hand moving roughly through her short strands. "I liked it long, but this suits you. You cut it because of Leather, didn't you? He always made you wear it in braids. I couldn't wait to feel it free and soft upon my hands—"

"A short cut is more practical," she said, defending herself. Piercing her ears and cutting her hair weren't much of a show for independence, but they mattered to her.

A moment later, he was crouching beside her, jerking socks onto her feet that were warm and too large. He stood slowly, looking down at her solemnly. "It isn't worth it, Gwyneth. You'll kill yourself if you keep this up. Sell the ranch, lease it, but don't try to fill Leather's dream with your life."

"Don't lecture me, Tanner. It's homestead land and—"

She sneezed and he held a tissue to her nose. "Blow."

She did, resenting his upper hand at the moment as the storm battered the house, leaves slashing the window screens. Lightning outlined Tanner's powerful body as he stood watching nature's fierce display. He looked too alone, as if life had slammed into him too many times, taking away the happy youth she'd known.

"What did I do to you?" Gwyneth watched a ladybug crawl across the white peony bouquet he'd stuck ruthlessly into an old blue glass canning jar. He would probably remember how Anna always had fresh flowers on the table, honoring his mother. His question, the one circling her days, haunting her nights, slid so quietly into Anna's comfortable kitchen, that it sounded louder than the storm outside. *"Do you know what you've done to me, Gwyneth—sweet little Gwynnie? Done to me...done to me..."*

He turned to her, his face in the shadows as he leaned against the kitchen counter. "I did it to myself," he said softly, lightning outlining his broad shoulders, his muscled neck.

"What do you want from me?" she heard herself ask

unevenly, her whisper louder than the raging storm outside.

"I want you to stay until morning. From the look of your old roof, the ceiling is probably dripping now."

"Obligation to you isn't a good fit, Tanner Bennett. Neighbors here return favors." His clothing gathered her up, warm and safe inside it, as she sipped the tea and felt its comfort. There was no safety or comfort in the same room as her ex-husband, for from the set of his jaw, he was determined upon his course. She'd seen that same expression when he played sports. He homed in on an idea, focused and went for it.

She had the uncomfortable feeling that she was the object of his game now.

"There are those who do not care one way or the other about the Rules for Bride Courting, or the way a man and a woman choose each other," he said softly, crossing his arms over his chest. "We skipped that part, the first time."

The flex of his shoulders, his forearms across that lightly furred triangle on his chest, did little to give her peace. Her fingertips moved on the cloth napkin, embroidered with Anna's daisies, and Gwyneth wondered how it would feel to run her fingers through that spot, just there, over his heart. How it would feel, that small enticing line of hair as her touch prowled lower, to just there, where his navel rested secretly. And lower to that... He'd never touched her breast, cupped it in his hand, and she wondered at how it would feel, trusting him with her body, letting him fill her.

"Our lives stopped back then. We let others tear us apart." His low, soft voice terrified her, her hand shaking as it brought the cup to her lips.

The clatter of the cup into the saucer caused her to shiver. "That time is gone now, Tanner."

"Is it?" he asked in a curt way that took a sudden heat dancing along her body, already warm within his clothing. "You kissed me hard, Gwyneth, as if you'd waited, and couldn't wait a minute more. You tasted of sweet desperation. Did you? Did you think of how it would be, not only the loving, but the life we could have had, those babies held close and loved between us? Did you think of how it would be on a stormy night like this when we'd be holding each other snug and warm and safe?"

She'd dreamed of him…erotic dreams in which he'd moved over her, filled her, stroked and heated her body with his kisses. She despised the telling blush that moved up from her throat and prayed the night's shadows would hide her thoughts from him.

"It was only a kiss. There's a part of Anna in you—" The lie crackled around her.

He chuckled at that. "That was no fond, remembering-my-mother kiss. You flung your arms around me and took. You were hungry, sweetheart. I barely escaped you tossing me to the ground and—"

"Why are you here?" she asked in a shaky whisper, rising to her feet, and placing the chair between them as he walked toward her in the shadowy kitchen.

"Because I want it finished. I have to know that if we'd made the whole journey, if I'd have given you time and we'd followed the rules every step, and I hadn't pushed you, we… I have to know that it couldn't have worked, wouldn't have worked, if we'd tried and gone through the steps, one by one. Don't you ever think about that? What would have happened?"

She gripped the back of the chair until her hands

ached. She couldn't forget those men tearing at her, nor could she forget Tanner walking to her bed that night. "Sometimes closure doesn't come. It can't."

"It can," he murmured and skimmed a finger along her ear, circling it warmly before tugging the lobe. "You can kiss me now, if you like. Just put your mouth on mine and show me that you're not afraid of what could happen between us."

"You want to go back. That isn't possible. I'm not twenty to your twenty-four anymore. We're both bitter in our ways."

She stood very still, breathing hard, as his rough cheek rested along hers, intimate and yet not pressing. "Not back. Forward. We'd have aged anyway and it's time to clear out the cobwebs that remain. We're different now, I admit. But there's something there that hasn't changed. Are you afraid to make the journey with me, to find the truth?"

His open mouth cruised along her skin, burning her, yet not pushing.

"This is your mother's house, Tanner Zachariah Bennett," she whispered, her tone lacking the indignation she sought. What was the heat burning her, his bare chest so close to hers? How would all that power and heat and texture feel against her?

"You're sexy, Mrs. Bennett, and you're shaking and warm. We've got to make certain you're not ill, don't we? My mother would understand." His lips pressed gently at the corner of hers, then drifted to the other side. "Mmm. There's a bit of fever there, I think."

She shivered as his lips eased along her cheek and drifted lower to her throat, opening on her skin. "Fever there, too, a fast-beating pulse."

She was breathing hard now, sucking air into her

lungs, and filling them with his scent. She closed her
eyes, captured by his warmth, his gentle kisses along her
skin. "Ask me to the dance, Gwyneth," he whispered
against her parted lips and she found her fingers locked
on his strong upper arms. Though he wasn't touching
her, other than his lips, she couldn't bear for him to leave
her, her senses tangled with memories of a younger Tanner, and the man so near her now. Perhaps it was true,
that fever ran within her—for she gave herself to his
kiss and let the past float away....

Gwyneth awoke in Tanner's bedroom, the cloudy
morning peering through the curtains. Lying amid the
high school trophies, the footballs and baseball bats and
gloves, the high school pictures framed on the wall, she
closed her eyes and ached with the sweetness of his
kisses.

And that last one—hard, exciting, knowing one of a
man who desired a woman. Long ago, he'd kissed her,
his body trembling next to hers, but he'd always been
so gentle. The last kiss, his lips parted over hers, nudging
hers open. She'd had the feeling of jumping off a very
safe cliff into unchartered waters that swept her away.
The intimacy of his tongue had shocked her, and then it
came, that hard, fierce kiss, the claiming.

The claiming. Tanner wanted to finish that night, to
make love to her, to finish what rose hot and trembling
between them.

With the broody morning hovering outside, she shivered beneath the quilt marked by Anna's neat stitches
and caught his scent. There was nothing tender in his
eyes when he'd lifted his head and she'd found herself
clinging to him, leaning against him. For in all that time,

he had not touched her...had not touched her, only the sweetness of his lips on hers.

The scent of damp grass and fragrant flowers drifted around her. She couldn't bear to face him this morning, not after she'd sought his mouth, hungered for him, felt the heat burn in her.

She inhaled roughly, smoothing the worn, soft sheets. *All the time they kissed, the hot, leaping current between them, he hadn't touched her.*

Turning her head to see the time, she saw that it was already nine o'clock and she hadn't gathered the eggs or fed the dogs. But they were safe, in Tanner's boat building. She tested her body, a lingering ache from the chill last night, and another ache she didn't want to define, a hunger that couldn't be— *"Did you think of how it would be, not only the loving, but the life we could have had, those babies held close and loved between us? Did you think of how it would be on a stormy night like this when we'd be holding each other snug and warm and safe?"*

Then she saw his dresser, sunlight skimming through the clouds to flash upon broken glass, a framed picture of their wedding day, with her tucked close against him.

Ten minutes later, she found him in his boat shop, glad that she hadn't had to face him in the house. It was only good manners to thank him for caring for her dogs and for her. *He'd held her against him, sleeping bag and all, sheltering her from the cold rain, her head tucked beneath his chin as he ran, and she'd never felt so safe.*

Caught by the sight of him shaving with a straight razor, bare to the waist, strips of his jaw foamy with soap and the other gleaming and shaven, she tried to move and couldn't. The way he locked his jeaned legs apart, and set his strong body down to his canvas deck shoes caused her heart to leap. She wondered how that hard haunch would feel beneath her hand. The cloudy day let just enough light into the building to skim his body, gleam upon it and make her fingers itch to stroke that tanned skin....

His glance ripped down her clothing, freshly washed and dried, down to his borrowed work boots, far too large for her feet. "I—my boots are out here," she heard herself say. When she could tear her eyes away from the droplets of water clinging to the hair on his chest, his tanned skin a contrast to the white towel around his neck, she saw his neatly made cot in a corner of the building. "I didn't notice that before."

"You were too busy telling me to stay out of your business. I slept there, if that's what you're wondering. I'm not about to sleep in Mother's room, or that frilly mess of ruffles in my sisters' rooms. I doubt Mother's couch would withstand the first good toss, and that's what I've been doing lately—tossing and missing sleep." He swished the razor in the basin's soapy water and began to shave, a fascinating process to Gwyneth. Leather had used an electric razor and the old-fashioned method Tanner used was one she'd seen his father use, a man indulging the curiosity of little girls. Tanner would do the same, adding a swipe or two for an elegant show, letting little girls gape at him from the bathroom door, and then soaping their jaws and sending them out to play.

Tanner was bred to be a family man, to have a home and cuddle babies.

She forced her eyes away again, taking in the rows of bookshelves, the area masculine and spartan when compared to Anna's doilies and treasured antique furniture. Tanner didn't fit into the house now, and missing his

mother—oh, how Gwyneth ached for Anna, to be able
to talk with her. To be truthful, Anna's telling journal
had angered her, and it still did. Her life could have been
safe, without Tanner, flowing without painful secrets
opened and—

She inhaled the fresh scent of coffee and drooled, not
wanting to ask him for more, her stomach clenching
from hunger. She'd be on her way soon enough, just
after she said thank-you and goodbye.

He'd be missing his mother, aching for her in the
same way, if not more. He'd come out here, built himself
a corner to rest, for inside the house, memories of Anna
were too dear.

Gwyneth glanced at her dogs, dozing comfortably,
and wanted to run away—instead she found herself looking at the large boat plans tacked along the wall. She
wondered about his life away from the valley, how he
could have traveled so far and done so much. Tanner
came to stand beside her, wearing a white T-shirt, neatly
tucked into his waistband. Everything about him was so
neat and in its place now, a far distance from the carefree
boy that he was. He handed her a mug of coffee and a
sweet roll from Eli's Bakery, stuffed with raspberry jam.
"Eli came by this morning. He forgot JoAnn's birthday
and wants to build a boat for her. She's Norwegian and
sometimes her sea blood calls to her, though he doesn't
like the water. This one is small, shallow and light and
easy, a good choice for her. A Norwegian pram. Good
for fishing in smooth water."

He rubbed his jaw, a smile flirting along his lips. "He
wants a carved dragon's head, like a Viking ship, and
the mix won't set well on a pram, weighing it down.
We'll see. I think we could do something with Viking
designs along the side instead."

He pointed to another plan, tacked on the wall, marked with blue lines and measurements. "A double-paddle canoe. That's a sea kayak, and that, a biscayne bay, fast and easy to handle, a good lake sailer. I can see you in that."

With a nudge of his elbow, he took her down to another plan. "This is the love of my heart, the skiff. Four lapstrake—layered along the sides, flat bottomed, meant to last, easy to scull…to oar. Have you ever sculled, matching the rhythm of your oar to another's, Gwyneth?"

The coffee scalded her lips and so did the sultry look in Tanner's eyes as another rhythm, that of bodies matching pace, burned into her mind. "You know I haven't…how did you learn all this?" He'd been so far away, had so many experiences, while she'd sat still in her life, tangled in paying bills and fighting what couldn't be. Why would he want to come back, to re-open the past and hurt them both?

"From a tough Norwegian with a top boatyard on the Pacific. I worked with him, learned from him, and eventually bought him out." He bent to take a quick kiss and the sweetness lingered as he walked away, the scent of soap and man curling around her.

"How could you just do that, pick up and decide you didn't want to teach school, that you wanted to go to sea?" she asked, tasting the raspberry sweet roll and then finishing it hungrily. She looked at all the books, the boat models that he'd probably built, and knew that once Tanner had set his mind to a task, he would finish it.

"I wanted the salt and sea air to wipe away what was dark and aching inside me. It's a busy life on board, especially during a squall or a storm at sea. I liked that, pitting myself against nature. Now I'm wanting something else. I'm wanting peace. Working with my hands, feeling the wood live beneath my touch, is one way.''

The image of harsh ocean waves closing over him as he drowned terrified her. ''You could have drowned. What about your mother? How would she have felt? You and Kylie and Miranda were her heart.''

How would she have felt, if he'd been taken away? How much more guilt and loss could she bear?

He turned away from her, looking out into the broody morning, the rain having flattened his mother's herb garden, dripping like tears around the buildings. He stood so alone, and the crush of loneliness and grief filled the air. She wanted to go to him, to put her arms around him, to comfort him, for Anna had been torn away too soon. Instead, because habit locked her feet still, she ached for him and ran her finger around the rim of the coffee mug. ''She knew you loved her, Tanner.''

He said nothing, but the muscles of his neck tensed as did his fists hanging loosely at his side. In his eyes was a haunting that matched the emptiness of his voice. ''I wasn't here. She had so little.''

''She had so much.''

He stood still, her heart aching for him, for Anna. Gwyneth wanted to give him peace, the closure he needed to deal with his loss. She foraged for what she could give him and found nothing served the task. She heard the hurried beating of her heart and heard herself speak. The words came from her heart and not her mind, startling her. ''Would you come to the Sweetheart Dance with me?''

He remained still and she prayed he hadn't heard—then he turned and walked slowly to her, his face in the shadows. Looming over her, Tanner's expression was hard, lines drawn beside his firm mouth and between his brows. "Don't pity me, Gwynnie. I won't have it. Don't sacrifice yourself in sympathy. Because my mother has nothing to do with what runs between us."

A hot storm of hunger ran through her now and only Tanner was a part of it, his body calling to hers. She couldn't hold him; she'd tossed away that right years ago and she wasn't certain of herself now. "I have no intention of doing that. You said you wanted to know if things would have been different. You'll see, they would have ended poorly. But if it's that you need, I—"

"Oh, I need more than that. You took my pride, Mrs. Bennett, a man who couldn't keep his bride on their wedding night."

"You know why." Her words echoed in the spacious room and her dogs whined, sensing the humans' tension.

He ran a finger down her hot cheek, studying her. "Eli noticed your dogs and your boots beside them. He saw your sleeping bag drying over the sawhorses. By now, you and I have stirred up quite a few untruths, I'd say."

"You're being difficult. You wanted to go to the dance, to have your pound of flesh, and you have my offer. Take it or leave it." With that, unable to bear more, she tromped in his large boots to her own. She plopped down on her dogs' blanket and unlaced the boots, tearing them off as she would like to remove Tanner from her thoughts. She jammed on her boots and stood. She shook her head, disbelieving that she could have opened her mouth and asked him to the dance, a formality for women who wanted and accepted the man courting her. "It doesn't mean anything, only to those who want to marry by Freedom Valley's customs. Anyone can go to a dance, Tanner—anyone. Years ago, you took me, but I knew you weren't concerned with customs and at the time, I didn't care. It's the ice cream contest that draws most of them, not the last dance when they'll take home their intended sweethearts.''

"You take me, and I'll be wanting that last dance," he said quietly, measuring her across the shadowy building, tension humming between them.

She threw out her hands as his smile became a boyish grin, enough to flip her heart and take away her breath. "Look, we'll just go. I'll see that the Cull label gets taken off you. I can do that, at least. We'll do this recourtship thing if it's so important to you, and somewhere along the line, you'll fail a test, or I will, or you'll just come to your senses. That way, you won't be branded a Cull and if you decide to marry and keep the valley's customs with another woman, and it's important to her—''

"For the good of another woman, you'd suffer, is that it?'' he asked too softly and too carefully. "Passing me along, handing me down to another woman, so you won't have to deal with me?''

Another woman. The words echoed coldly around her. She didn't want to think of Tanner capturing another woman with just his kisses as he had last night. "The whole thing is futile. Everyone will know it's a sham. I'm not going so far as the marriage.''

She knew wearily from that dark, narrowed look that Tanner was out to finish his journey and drag her along with him; she knew it would be a battle to make him back down.

"From what I remember, there's the trial marriage first, living in the same house and an inspection by the Women's Council to see if I'm up to par.''

"You won't make it that far. You know the steps—

first you'll have to stand in front of the Women's Council and give them your intentions. You wouldn't dare—''

"It's only words, Gwyneth, dear heart. I can give them what they want. That's what you did that day we married, wasn't it? Spoke vows you didn't intend to keep?"

His bitter, deep tone clawed at her and she eyed him, not wanting to give an inch of her freedom. She'd been bound by one man, trapped by his illness and love. "They'll see through you. They'll know what you're doing, making me pay for running out that night."

When he lifted his eyebrows, questioning her, she threw up her hands again. "Well?" she demanded finally, furious with herself and with him for looking so pleased. "Are you going to the dance with me, or not?"

"Okay," he said lightly as though she had just asked him if he wanted another cup of coffee. He picked up a plank of wood, studying it, running his hands over it as though he were already building boats, forgetting her. "You'll have to pick me up in a surrey and take me to the dance, you know."

"You've got a month to change your mind before the Sweetheart Dance in late July," she said, temper rising. "You'll have to stand up the week before and look foolish while they ask you questions."

"Maybe, but then we'll know for sure, won't we? Who can stand and who can't?" Tanner jerked up his safety glasses and then his power saw was ripping through seasoned planks as if he had cut through the safety of her life.

Five

They ate all my pies, set to cool on the back picnic table. The boys are playing baseball in the cow pasture now, some of them with eyes on my daughters, Kylie and Miranda, and showing off outrageously. Having sense, my girls and Gwyneth Smith won't have anything to do with them. But there will come a day for all of them, when love comes calling.

—Anna Bennett

"Your ex-wife looked like a first-class thunderstorm when I passed her in town, old buddy," Gabriel Deerhorn said as he sprawled on one lawn chair and propped his worn moccasins on another in Anna's backyard. The third week of July was a fine time for a late-afternoon football game in the pasture, a solid session of grunt and sweat, and a men's barbecue in the backyard. Gabriel took a long sip of iced tea and watched Tanner tend the steaks and foil-wrapped potatoes cooking on the barbecue grill. "Nice to have someone else's cooking. Make mine rare. So you're going before the Women's Council this week, are you?"

Tanner had had a month of Gwyneth's dark looks and silence. She was circling him, confident that her icy mood would derail him from appearing in front of the Women's Council and stating his intentions. Oh, he'd be there all right.

Tanner inhaled the fresh evening air, scented with his mother's flowers and herbs. He'd missed this, sharing an evening with his friends, sprawled on lawn chairs in Anna's backyard and waiting to be fed. Throughout the years, they'd come together like this, a blend of immigrant and Native American heritage, their names reflecting those roots. In Freedom Valley, it was custom to remember heritages, and so children were often tagged with names from the Bible and ones more common in other lands. Tanner glanced at Gwyneth's van barreling down the road. "Want to come? It's an open meeting. You can be my cheering section."

"No, thanks. I'll stick to my mountains. They're safer. I like my life," he said, a man who needed little and reminded those who knew him of his mountain man ancestor. Dressed in worn jeans and an unbuttoned chambray shirt, Gabriel's dark skin marked his Native American ancestry. He dusted a bit of pasture dirt from his jeans. "You tried this once. Take care of her, Tanner. She's not up to your experience."

Tanner lifted an eyebrow at the man who would protect Gwyneth. "I won't harm her. But she's got thorns now and she wouldn't want you defending her."

The men sitting around the picnic table and in lawn chairs shuttered slightly, all bearing scars of the Women's Council. They knew the power of the countryside's women, once banded together. More than one husband had been banned from his marriage bed and supper table for not taking a women's issue seriously. Single men who had offended the Women's Council drew smaller shares at Willa's Wagon Wheel Café, and were avoided by husbands who were warned off by their wives. Single men who had not offended the Council ate well and were courted casserole and pie-style by women looking for husbands. Tanner was on borrowed time in Freedom Valley, the dishes on his table were a welcome-home to Anna's son. The flow would eventually stop, dropping him back into the Cull bin. One wrong move and the supply would instantly be cut off.

Tanner expertly turned the foil-wrapped baked potatoes on the new supersize grill he'd just purchased from Livingston's Hardware Store. Gwyneth had come into the store, noted him with all the affection of a deer caught by headlights, and had turned briskly, hurrying away. So much for an interested woman. "I always liked a good stormy sea. Makes the crossing more interesting."

"You've caught it. That nesting urge. The next thing you know, you'll be baby-sitting for twins and she'll be saying no to any get-togethers like this one. Women set hard rules," Gabriel muttered, looking off into the mountains rising in the distance. There he wouldn't have to think of anything but fishing and the sweet fresh air and highland meadows. "I'll be damned if I'll jump to the Rules of Bride Courting. You won't find me led around with a ring through my nose."

"No one says we have to do it, go through the whole

silly mess. We can date who we want and marry without that fandango," York Meadows said around a mouthful of Emma Mae Bradford's potato salad.

Michael Cusack, wearing motorcycle boots, black jeans and a black T-shirt, lay on the picnic table's bench, his arms behind his head. Raised by a drunken and heavy-handed father, and in trouble before he was twelve, Michael had seen the darker side of life and didn't want emotional ties of any kind. Anna had taken him in, stuffed him with good food when she could, and had loved him. In return, he cherished her with what was left of his heart. Anna's daughters were the only girls he'd left alone, which had angered them both. "You're not in my league, kid," he'd told sixteen-year-old Kylie. To Miranda, he'd said, "Give it a rest. Your high-class backside wouldn't suit the oil on my motorcycle."

Tanner flipped a burger. Kylie and Miranda had promised to come back and help him disassemble their mother's household and possessions and there was certain to be fireworks. When Kylie and Miranda were sweetheart-shopping, they'd brushed romantically with several of Tanner's friends, but nothing had come of the brief flirtations except his sisters' fierce "detestation of immature, pants-too-tight and heads-too-big male animals." As opposite as his sisters were, they agreed on one topic—that the now adult members of the Bachelor Club were swaggering, despicable and arrogant, too lowly to be thought of as marriage material.

"It's a bunch of bunk," Michael said now. "You won't catch me dancing to that Women's Council's tune. Women take me or leave me."

"Uh-huh," Dakota Jones said disbelievingly. "The way women have come and gone at your house for the last three years, they're mostly leaving. Funny that no one seems to know anything about them.'' The owner of a sporting goods store, now that his parents had retired, Dakota charmed his female customers but kept free of romantic entanglements. His unmarried sister, Karolina Jones, alias ''Super Snoop,'' was considered his only redeeming quality. His mother's open affairs hadn't given him a good picture of female fidelity. ''Women around here are used to being treated special. They stick together like a covey of quail. All except Gwyneth who married Tanner without anyone's blessings. She paid plenty for that, too, my friend. You left town, but she had to face them every day after that and I don't imagine Leather made her life easy, either.''

Tanner frowned, studying the sizzling steaks. ''I'm sorry about that. I should have given her more time.'' He'd pushed her, desiring her and a new life, too hurried to give her the time she needed. In a way, he was as much of a bully as old Leather. Tanner had heard that Leather had used his terminal illness to run Gwyneth night and day. A soft woman, she wouldn't have resisted and probably had worked all day and nursed all night.

''Life rolls on,'' noted Fletcher Rowley, once a rookie in the pro baseball leagues until his bad knees brought him home to Freedom. He'd taken over his father's small-engine repair business; and he was happy to be living in a tiny apartment attached to the ramshackle business. Fletch took what life offered; his ex-wife hadn't taken his baseball failure well and had moved on to another successful player. The only thing Fletch mourned after the divorce was his baseball cards, which she had burned.

Dakota tossed one of Esmeralda Dormay's frosted nut brownies in the air and caught it in his teeth, not both-

ering to use his fingers as he finished it. ''They've never
forgiven us for forming the Bachelor Club when we
were younger. The time has come for me to be a daddy,
men, and I'm not letting that bunch of women pick me
over. I've got the nesting urge and they know it. I'm
signing up for one of those dating services and hunting
outside the herd.''

The rest of the men all looked at him and Dakota, a
rogue with a reputation for hot lips and no commitments,
lifted his brows. ''What? I want kids. I'm getting old.
My swimmers may be getting weak and I want to let
them have a chance to do their job. My sister's kids have
done their magic on me. So what? If that dating gig
doesn't work, I'll adopt.''

''Hey. We grew up together. Let us not malign our
swimmers,'' Michael Cusack noted disdainfully.

''Deserter,'' York muttered. ''Married men don't eat
like this, and they've got to deal with frost and cold
shoulders and headaches if they step the wrong way. I've
been married. Food wasn't the problem,'' York said
darkly, shielding the old pain that shot through him. He
would have loved his baby, paid his wife to keep it full-
term, but Margo had other plans and none of them in-
cluded ruining her figure.

Tanner glanced at Gwyneth's van tearing back up the
road. From the shadowy window, she glared at him. Tanner lifted his hand to his mouth and blew her a kiss. The
van skidded to a stop, reversed and Gwyneth pulled into
Anna's lane, stopping in the driveway. She marched to
him, wearing a battered T-shirt beneath her cutoff bib
overalls. All of the men stood to their feet as their mothers had taught them to do—for in Freedom Valley, even
as boys they knew that poor manners would cut off their
supply of chocolate cake and ice cream.

"Gentlemen." The words, "pigs" and "beasts" curled around Gwyneth's cool tone, for she shared Kylie and Miranda's opinion of the adult "Bachelor Club." Her hazel eyes scathed Fletch's dirtied, battered shirt, the holes in his grass-stained jeans, his too-long hair. She glared at the men's smiles until they died and they sat quietly, hunkering uncomfortably now in their pasture dirt, sweat and bachelor status. Satisfied that she'd put them in their lowly places, she studied the expensive grill, the bratwursts and steaks, and glared at Tanner, her hands on her hips. "That's quite the macho toy—can it fly? May I speak to you in private?"

"Certainly, my love. Steaks and burgers are ready, so go ahead and stuff yourselves," Tanner said to his friends. He appreciated the long line of her legs and the fast sway of her hips as she preceded him into his boat building. He'd waited for her to come calling, to blast him for clearing away the tree limb that had crashed through her rooftop; an independent woman, she probably didn't appreciate the repair of the roof, either.

She turned on him, panic filling her hazel eyes, and he wanted to hold her close, to cherish her all the more. *"I can't do it."* Her rushed words bounced around the spacious cool building, the skeletal board form upon which a high-priced skiff would be born.

Tanner jammed his hands into his back pockets and watched her storm, tramping in front of his bed. He wanted her in it, under him. But he'd pushed a young girl last time and now he'd settled in for a long haul, taking his time. "Okay," he agreed lightly. "Whatever you want."

"Okay? Just okay? Forget about it?" She came up close to him, so close he could catch her scent beneath that of potter's clay and hay and gasoline. She peered up at him. "You're letting it drop, just like that? Good. Then you've realized how foolish this whole thing is."

"Uh-huh. It's up to you what happens. I knew you'd back out," he said, watching the dim light catch in her hair like tiny sparks.

She frowned up at him, studying his expression. "I don't trust you. You're not an easy man now, Tanner. You've got too much locked up inside you. You kissed me. Hard and hot and hungry. Why?"

He shrugged, pushed away the knowing smile lurking at his mouth and watched her plow through her confusion. "I do not have a hope chest this time, either, Tanner, and you know it's the custom for a woman to have a hope chest filled with pillowcases, tea towels and such. I don't have time for embroidery, even if I knew how."

"Fine with me." He tried not to wince as Gwyneth's fist grabbed his black T-shirt and a few hairs on his chest.

"Don't start with me, Tanner Zachariah Bennett. I know that innocent look. I've known you all my life. We'd have to go through the steps, live together—*live together.*"

"Then we'd know, wouldn't we?" he asked quietly. "We'd know if it could have worked."

"Oh, yes, we'd know. What if you kiss me like that again? What if all of me goes all hot and quivery again, and—?" She hurriedly placed her hand over her mouth and looked up at him, horrified that she'd spoken her thoughts. She studied his mouth, with a dark, shielded hungry tigress look, and his body went hard.

There in the filtered light, a trembling heat and hunger swirled around them. It danced on his senses, slammed into Tanner's stomach and lodged in his bunched muscles. He noted the fear and the curiosity in her expres-

sion, and the tiny lick of her tongue upon her lips gave
her away.

"Put your arms around me and kiss me, Gwyneth. I
won't move. I won't touch you. It's your choice."
Would she trust him enough to come to him, place her
body against his and taste the dreams they both could
have had?

Her warring emotions played across her face and then
just when he ached for one touch to keep him alive and
warm, she wrapped her arms around his neck and pushed
her mouth against his.

He stood, unmoving, rock hard and safe, his hands in
his pockets. She tossed away the fear that came stalking
her, her need to feed upon Tanner's mouth was greater
than the familiar nightmares. She dived her hands into
his thick hair, reveled in its warmth as it flowed through
her fingers; she gloried in the slight scrape of his skin
against her own, her mouth angling for a tighter fit. She
tasted his iced tea, the hard, intriguing line of his lips,
the scent of sun-dried clothing and smoke on him; she
tasted the mystery, the excitement, the heat lurking beneath, tempting her to come calling—

The beat of his heart quickened, pushing against her
breasts, summoning her skin to heat with his, and yet he
hadn't moved, except to bend his head lower, to better
meet her mouth. "You can put your arms around me,"
she heard herself whisper over the pounding of her heart.

"Say that again," he rasped deeply, unevenly, as if
he couldn't believe what he had heard.

That delighted her, that Tanner, so confident and
strong, would question himself with her, as if she had
some secret power over him. Was this how it was to feel
like a woman? To know that strength waited inside her,
for her bidding? "Do it," she whispered, opening her

lips to run them over the rough skin of his chin. "Hold me."

In a heartbeat, his arms were around her, pressing her close, lifting her higher to his mouth. The heat rushed between them, burning her, and his big hands opened over her bottom, cupping her, pushing her close to his rigid, hard body. She could feel the heat throbbing from him, stunned by her own melting body, the softness within her, and the ache deep, deep inside pulsing almost painfully. His tongue moved rhythmically with hers and, suckling him, she wanted more. Her lower body, just there between her thighs, clenched moistly, aching...

She wanted him in her, filling her.

She jerked her head back from his mouth, studied the burning heat of his eyes, the rigid lock of his jaw. She pushed air into her lungs, tasting him on her lips, upon her tongue, as he held her close, breast to chest, heat to heat. She had to have him touch her, burn her—

"Touch me." In the distance, her voice was a rasp, low and husky and unsteady.

The rough, dark sound that came cruising up his throat wrapped around her enticingly. She anchored her hands to his safe shoulders, preventing him from escaping. The shocking storm vibrated between them and all her dreams lurked nearby. While his fiercely intense expression fascinated her, he cupped her bottom, lifting her feet off the ground. He carried her into the privacy of the building's sheltered corner, the shadows near his cot, away from the open windows and the steady rumbling voices of the men. He opened the snaps of her bib overalls, one by one; his dark gaze raked hotly down to her breasts. The tremor that ran through Tanner's muscled body shook her own as he placed both big hands on the light cotton cloth covering her and gently caressed the softness.

She couldn't keep from sighing, because the dreams were true. Sweet soft dreams, not the ugliness. With a groan that sounded as though he'd kept it locked up for years, Tanner lifted her to his mouth and the moist heat of his mouth tugged at her breast.

She cried out, shaking, unprepared for the delight that ran from her breasts hotly down to her lower belly. The shocking jolt continued, her body clenching, again and again and she whirled out into her own world, fresh and clean amid the bursting stars.

"Gwyneth…Gwyneth…" Tanner's rough low voice vibrated against her hot cheek, his body throbbed against hers, but she only had time to feel, to step into the glorious new delight that went on and on—

With a rough, hushed sound, filled with hunger, Tanner lowered her body to his cot and she couldn't stop the twisting of her hips, the soft cries that churned around her. She found his mouth in the shadows, felt it open hot and hungry on her, just as she'd dreamed. And then she gave herself to the dream—his bare chest against her breasts, slightly rough, skimming her nipples with his kisses as the fever ran on, hurling her down an almost painful passage of delight. She instinctively raised her hips to his cupping hand, unable to prevent the high keening sound of need escaping her. The tugging of his mouth sent her higher and then he touched her, just there, stroked her and she spun off into the blaze of heat and sparks, her body tightening and tightening and throbbing around his touch until she burst free.

Lying on his side beside her, Tanner was shaking, his face hot against her cheek, his hands gentle and soothing upon her trembling body, rearranging her clothing.

He'd touched her intimately. She hadn't been terrified
The world was still soft and quiet in the building, the
shadows curling around her.

Tanner raised to look down at her, his hand leisurely
smoothing her breast. "You sounded as if—" He swallowed and looked away. "Don't let this frighten you,
Gwyneth. It's only—"

Only! Her body still quivered at his touch. *Only!* Deep
inside she still ached, and a final, stunning contraction
sent her flat against the bed, eyes wide-open, gasping for
breath as she centered on that lovely peak deep within
her.

Tanner growled and slowly raised to prop himself
against the wall, studying her.

"I can't move," she managed to say, gasping for
breath. She wanted to leap to her feet, fly to safety where
she could probe what had happened in her, with Tanner,
and where she could tuck that feeling away. "Go have
dinner with your friends, and I'll just rest here a while."

His hand stroked her upper thigh, just there on the
inside and another quiver ran through her. "You think I
can move?" he asked ruefully.

"This isn't funny," she whispered. She tried to move
and her hands flopped at her sides. "I'm all in a puddle
here, all warm and gooey and I don't know where my
bones have gone. Now that's an awful thing to do to a
woman."

His brows shot up and laughter curled his lips. "Awful?"

"I'm humming inside," she said desperately, trying
to understand what had happened to her. She wanted to
trace that beguiling line beside his mouth, but couldn't
summon the strength. "Stop grinning before I hit you."

Tanner took her limp hand and kissed the palm. His

fingers tightened on her thigh. "Oh, you're warm all right and you're 'humming.' Correction—you're hot. You just exploded, Gwyneth-mine. You respond like a firecracker."

"This is awful. What are we going to do about it?" she asked, trapping the fingers that were tracing designs higher and higher on her leg.

"I don't know," he said rawly. "It pays to be careful."

Careful? she thought, panicked. Where was "careful" a moment ago? "We can't just walk out there. They'll know. You're all hot-looking."

His look at her was one of pure disgust. "I am hot and I am very hard. And yes, dammit, they will know."

"Oh." Just that inadequate little "oh" was all she could muster from the shattering she'd just experienced. "Maybe I could help?" She looked down to the proof of his desire, straining against his jeans. She reached to touch him, to explore what she'd wanted to hold, what she'd held in her dreams, burning her palm, fitting close against her.

He frowned grimly at her. "Do not touch me now, Gwyneth."

"It wouldn't have fit," she said, staring at the blunt pressure beneath the snap of his jeans. Those bad men had hurt her, tearing her apart, but Tanner's body was much larger. She shuddered, because she knew his big hands would have made short work of them, and it would have been murder in his eye, when he went after them.

Had she really held him close moments ago? Did he really touch her, like that? Was that how men touched women, with gentle reverence and leashed hunger and simmering heat, with hearts pounding and hands shaking?

He inhaled shakily. "Were you scared? Of me? Touching you?"

"It happened too fast. I didn't know it could happen that fast. I mean when the touching is good. In the movies—"

"You lost control, Gwyneth—" Tanner rubbed his forehead as if he were stunned, with a King Kong headache looming nearby. "I've got to lay here for a while. Move over."

The cot creaked beneath them as Tanner settled along her side. He gathered her against him, and placed her head on his shoulder. He seemed so vulnerable, needing time to regroup, and she wanted to comfort him, stroking his hair. Held close against Tanner, she turned to listen to his heartbeat, to the steady safety of it. "It's nice here," she whispered.

"Mm-hmm." He nuzzled her hair, and kissed her ear, then settled back down, stroking her back in a soothing way that took the last of the tension from her. "How would you like to go sculling down at the lake?" he asked, bringing her hand to his lips again. "There's a rhythm to it that's interesting. You have to work up to it, easy like, until the strokes go deep and light enough and they have to match—"

"Rowing. That's all you can think of when I don't have a hope chest, and the whole town knows you're coming to the Women's Council and the questions they'll ask? I've got my pride, Tanner Bennett. I'm a woman now, and I can't come to you with nothing, not that *I would come to you*…and I don't have time for rowing and playing, Tanner. I've got cattle to tend and my pottery business is taking off and—"

"Playing is a part of life, sweetheart. Rhythms and approaching important problems with slow and careful planning can be of great benefit in the long run," Tanner said wisely, before giving her one long, sweet kiss that lacked the heat she'd just leaped into.

Rhythms. His touch had gently stroked her, the rhythm enticing... *Rhythms. Bodies moving together. Tanner's over hers, entering her.* Hunger leaped within her, her leg lifting along his and startled, more than frightened, she flung herself back, her hands over her face.

"Ouch!" Tanner rubbed the eye her elbow had caught and studied her with his other. "Why, Mrs. Bennett," he said teasingly, "I do believe you're blushing."

She scampered across him, her hand burning when it accidentally touched his hard, hot length. She took one look down at him, lying there, his hands behind his head his T-shirt pulled up to reveal that intriguing navel, his hair rumpled from her fingers. She swallowed heavily and pulled up the bib overalls that were starting to sag, sliding down her hips. That dark flick of passion slid from him to lick at her nerves, heating her and making her damp. That was all it took, one wicked, knowing look. She fastened her overalls with shaking hands and tried not to look at Tanner again, for he was a pure, sinful invitation for a woman to leap on him—

And the shocking pulse sang deeply within her, to have him all, to know what could have been and now could never be— Then the low rumble of men's voices curled around her. "Oh, my. Oh, my, Tanner. They were just outside and we—"

His low chuckle followed her out the door and before Gwyneth could start her van, he appeared at her window with a pie plate stuffed with food. "If I'm going to be playing househusband, taking care of you, I might as well start now. You need to eat better.''

''I've been taking care of myself for a long time, Tanner,'' she said, but hunger snagged at her stomach and pride fell before her need to take the delicious-looking food. She settled it gingerly on the seat beside her and stared up at him; the shocking, sensual jolt hit her low in her belly. ''You won't last.''

''Try me,'' he murmured with a sexy grin that said the Women's Council test wasn't the only test run in their future.

Gwyneth studied Tanner, his big body taking up most of the horse drawn surrey, as they rode to the Sweetheart Dance and Ice-Cream Social. Tanner's brand-new ice-cream churn sat on the floor behind the front, covered in heavy toweling. The simple, old-fashioned hand churn—redwood style—didn't match his deluxe monster barbecue grill. He would know that if there was anything that could lower a man in the estimate of other Freedom males, it was to have a motorized ice-cream churn. Gwyneth's customary bag of potato chips and dairy dip was in the grocery sack on the back seat next to the beautiful hope chest he'd made for her.

The big walnut and brass chest with an ornate lock was beautifully styled along the lines of a camelback trunk, and lined in cedar. On the top, he'd added carved initials—*G.S.B.* ''You've got your hope chest,'' he'd said, hefting it into the back of the surrey when she'd stopped to pick him up earlier. His big hands had efficiently tied a series of mystical knots, whipping the rope around the seat, securing it before dropping a light kiss on her gaping mouth. The flick of his tongue sent her tumbling, trying to catch her breath and when she did, the scent of his lime aftershave tangled with that of a headier scent that was Tanner's alone. Her fingers tightened on the reins of the borrowed rig and horses and that heat that ran through her as Tanner settled back, one arm behind her seat, his hand caressing her upper arm, terrified her.

His brief smile at her was too innocent for the shocking declarations he'd made in front of the Women's Council: "I pledge my life to protect and love her and to see that life comes easier to her. I will always dance the last dance with her, and if she wants me to live with her, on her terms, I will do all that I can to make her happy. At that time, the Committee for the Welfare of Brides would be welcome to visit. When she is sick, I will tend her. When she is troubled, I offer my shoulder to lean upon and if I can help—when she wants—I will."

He had looked at the toughest of the women seated around the table, a spinster of ninety who had seen a good share of the marriage offers before the Council, Fidelity Moore. "I take the blame for the first time. All of it," he said. "I leave the choosing to Gwyneth, whatever she wants of me, in her own time. I welcome your input and your inspection of my courting of her, according to the Rules of Bride Courting. Because there is not another woman I would have, that I would want to share my life and my children. She has my heart and always has."

The elected president, Fidelity, had sighed. Mary Lou Ledbetter, Jasmine Thatcher and the rest had nodded approvingly in the silence, and then Dahlia Greer's lusty, low laughter filled the meeting room. One of the younger members of the Council, Dahlia had skipped the fairytale appeal of romance and shot straight to the sexy appeal of Tanner.

Gwyneth had stared at him, unable to speak. She hadn't made him welcome, and she was certain that up to the last minute, he'd change his mind. But he stood, straight and tall, and spoke the words as if they were his vows.

Now, as the two horses' hooves clattered against the cobblestones in front of the town hall, Gwyneth glanced at Tanner. His white dress shirt and gray slacks and gleaming black dress shoes would have cost more than any of her livestock at auction.

He rubbed her head again in that affectionate gesture and she shook him off. "Stop."

"The things you said, like I made your heart race just looking at me, and that when you dreamed, you saw your babies nursing at my breast. *My breast! Babies nursing!* I am on the Council, Tanner, and men just do not say things like that. 'I'd like to try again' would have served."

"But think of the time that it saved with Karolina Jones scribbling away at her yellow pad, lining up an interrogation. For a librarian who wants to be a private eye, she asks irrelevant and possibly embarrassing questions. She could have asked why I desire you and I'd have had to tell the truth in detail, possibly describing how your body feels in my hands. How tight and sweet you can be, that delicate little panting noise you make, and how I get hard just—"

Gwyneth fought the blush rising on her cheeks, still shocked by her response to him. She pressed her thighs together because as he teased her with that deep, sensual purr, her body had clenched deep inside. "Karolina has ambitions. She would have had to investigate your murder. You're out to embarrass me."

"They wanted the truth. I gave it to them. I think your breasts are beautiful, what I have seen of them, and the sounds you make when I kiss them—" He glanced down at Gwyneth's warning hand locked on his thigh. He placed his hand over hers. "Incredible sounds, Gwyneth, as if your soul was flying into a starburst. That was your first time, wasn't it, on the cot?"

Was that the horses' hooves clip-clopping on cobblestones, or was it the unsteady, hurried beat of her heart? She shuddered and remembered the contractions deep within her. She glanced at her hand, too near his manhood and remembered the heat and size pressed intimately against her. After her jolting experience on Tanner's cot, she'd undressed in the privacy of her bathroom, the mixed scent of her body and his was unfamiliar and shocking. "I don't want to talk about that."

Tanner's finger slowly stroked the back of her neck as she slowed the horses in front of the ancient hitching post. "The druggist told me that Sadie McGinnis was certain to ask me what methods of birth control I used. She thinks I might try to get you pregnant, so you'd have to marry me. She thinks I'm a landlocked pirate after your land."

"It's that earring. You had it off for the Women's Council, but it gives you a certain look, especially with that swagger of yours. And just maybe, because of the way you're acting, you are a pirate. You've got a way about you now that wasn't there before." Tanner was no longer the football hero, the grinning youth who dazzled her, though at times that dear image skimmed through her. He was a man who knew how to charm and who was set on sealing the past away.

Her past came alive in her dreams every night, Tanner's soft kisses mixed with terrifying pain.

"I'm older and wiser. We both are, and you've got a swagger of your own now, shapely in the starboard and port sides, stern and aft full curved and sweet for a man's two hands to sink into and anchor. It's the anchor lock, me deep in you that is riding us both, and not an easy storm to weather. You're tight and too new, and that's a hard fact for a man who's wanting dearly and quickly to place his oar in the lock."

Tanner's voice was hard, as though he didn't like stating his desire, but the lovely, rolling words did their magic, curling snugly around her. "Hush. You can't say things like that."

"It's in my heart," he said, just as darkly, taking her hand to his mouth to flick the palm with his tongue and finish it with a burning kiss.

Gwyneth looked away into the sunset, shielding her flush as she withdrew her hand, rubbing the burn of his lips against her own thigh. He stared at her hand, and she knew that he wanted to kiss her there and... She trembled, forcing away the intimate thought.

She'd already gotten Sadie's informational call on the benefits of birth control when males were greedy and on the hunt. "He's in heat, in season for siring a brood, if ever I saw a man ready for the job," Sadie had said earnestly. "Absolutely disgusting it is, the way those Bachelor Club boys act when they're onto a woman. I saw it when they were younger. But for the good standing of their mothers, we would have labeled them all 'Culls' at puberty. Rakes, all of them, hot and lusting, and probably wanting to impregnate any woman available, then go their own merry way. Though they've been quiet lately, Tanner's focus on you could stir them up. We've got more work to do in the Women's Council than we can manage now. If we have to start inspecting premarriages and I have to give birth control advice to every innocent woman those boys decide…''

Men. Male. Tanner. Gwyneth thought, and hoped she wasn't drooling as Tanner stepped down from the surrey. He stretched, his body outlined by the dying sun. Before she could pull her eyes away, he'd circled the surrey, hitched the reins and stood at her side, his arms lifted to help her down—just as though she were a fine lady. Anna had trained her son well, but the gleam in his dark eyes wasn't all gentleman, but more of the hungry rogue biding his time. His body tensed as he slowly took in her only dress, a black short basic, a prize she couldn't resist in the secondhand store, the black pumps matching it.

When she prepared to get out of the seat, her skirt hiked up, revealing the black lace of her thigh-high hose, the tiny rosette of her garter belt. The purchase was from the first pot she'd sold. She'd been high on success and craving just one bit of feminine lace. Tanner's big, rough hand shot to her thigh, strong fingers locking to it, as though he'd wanted her then and there, wanted to part her thighs and ease between them. The dark, fierce hunger stormed around the hard angular planes of his face, his jaw tense. In that heartbeat, she knew what he'd look like above her, powerful muscles bunched to enter her… She swallowed and in the next instant, Tanner jerked down her skirt, his expression one of disgust. ''You're shaking. I'm sorry. I shouldn't have frightened you.''

But she wasn't frightened now of the past, rather of herself and the need to leap on Tanner and feed the hunger within her. How could he raise that bit of feminine savagery so quickly, that hungry, licking flame within her?

She shuddered as Tanner placed his hands on her waist, and heat pounded at her as he allowed her to lightly slide down his body to the earth. "I'll be expecting that last dance," he whispered as he picked up the heavy ice-cream churn with both hands and grabbed her grocery sack with his teeth. They gleamed in the dying light, his grin that of a rogue. For all to see, Tanner would follow her into the dance as a properly trained husband-to-be. After her tug, an attempt at independence, Tanner released the sack to her. But his eyes flashed a warning that he wouldn't always be so easy, letting her have her way.

At the door, she paused and found her hand anchored to the back of his belt. He looked grim and she studied him, fascinated with her first hint of a man's jealousy, because that's surely what gleamed in Tanner's dark eyes. He stood straight, like a warrior, ready to protect what was his, a stance meant to declare that she was his and he would fight for her. He looked so elemental, so rigid in declaring the boundaries of— She blinked, stunned at the meaning of his look. He thought her so desirable that other men would want her, such a prize that he had to protect her.

The heady sense that she was all woman, appealing to men, caused her to smile and some instinct told her to lean slightly against him, to comfort his unsteady, fragile emotions. Gwyneth couldn't resist fluttering her lashes up at him. "They're usually hungry."

"They'd better not come poaching," Tanner muttered.

"There is plenty of food." This unexplored side of Tanner fascinated her. They weren't talking of food, but of what ran between them. She hadn't played games like this before and a heady excitement washed over her, the challenge of flirting with Tanner, raising his hackles, testing him.

"It's not food I'm concerned about. I spoke my piece about you years ago and they know it still holds. You're still wearing my name and that means you've made a choice, too. We'll see this one out, just you and me, and we'll see if the ship holds water, and then we'll both know the right of it."

He spoke so firmly and darkly, in a solemn telling mix of seaman and country dialogue, that he took her breath away. He'd spoken for her long ago, warning off the other single men, when she was just eighteen. That fact lifted her heart and sent it sailing. She couldn't resist lifting a finger to stroke his cheek, to test his grim expression and reveling in her first attempt at flirting with Tanner. As a girl, she hadn't tested what lay curled softly inside her; she'd been too happy that he'd wanted to be with her. They'd laughed and played and he'd treated her to gentle, leashed kisses that told her he cherished her, that she was safe.

But was it "safe" she wanted now? Or was it Tanner, the man? She studied him, licked her lips and remembered that hot, wild kiss of his lips, the firm pressure of his fingers on her thigh—

"I'm a dead man," Tanner muttered after considering her expression. His tone had all the fragility of a man who knew he could fall easily to a dangerous woman's touch.

A heady little zing went swirling around her. Dangerous? Appealing? Her? The thought knocked her sideways and came back to circle her before Tanner placed his hand on her head, waggled it and grinned. "You'll get a headache, thinking so hard."

Six

If they are right for each other, blood runs hot
and sweet and magical between a man and a
woman. When the time is ripe, one will claim the
other and the other will be glad of it. Then a
sweeter storm will come, one that lasts a lifetime.
—Anna Bennett

After the dance, Gwyneth promptly dumped Tanner at
Anna's driveway. The casserole Anna May Polinski had
thrust into his hands with a flirtatious smile said she
didn't care about Freedom's customs, or that his ex-wife
was sitting in the surrey beside him, strangling the reins.

"Get out," Gwyneth had said, not looking at him.
"Everyone saw us dancing the last dance, the way you
held and looked at me, and the rumors are probably flying now. The last dance is supposed to mean something,

not this sham.'' She'd glared at the casserole held on his
lap. ''I've got a hard day's work tomorrow and I have
to return this borrowed team and surrey on top of that.''

Tanner wanted to tug her to him and take her mouth
and make her purr his name. But he wouldn't—because
this time, Gwyneth was calling the rules and taking her
time to decide what she wanted.

Waiting for a stubborn woman wasn't easy on a man
who had always charted his own life.

She'd trembled in his arms that first dance, and he
couldn't let her go after that. She held her body a safe
distance from his, except for that last dance and then,
the softness of her came sweetly against him, fitting per-
fectly. He couldn't resist taking a light kiss, testing the
full curve of her lips.

But he hadn't expected the flame between them to
ignite so quickly, Gwyneth placing her hands along his
jaw and tethering him for her seeking kiss. Heat burned
from her, scorching him, and while the music played,
he'd moved her into a sheltered corner, where he could
hold that firm curved bottom in both hands, cupping her
up tight against him. Gwyneth had torn her mouth away,
her fingers digging into his upper arms. Her eyes had
been bright with passion, staring up at him, her lips
swollen with his kisses. ''Your mouth looks different,''
she'd said, panting enticingly.

''That's because yours has been sucking and nibbling
at it,'' he'd managed to say unsteadily and wondered if
he'd live through Gwyneth exploring her female powers.
She'd been trapped, years ago, just on the cusp of wom-
anhood and now was uncertain. It was a fine price he
was paying in her experiments, but gladly so.

''What are you doing?'' she'd asked with a frown,
squirming slightly within his hold.

"What are you?" he'd returned with a grin and caressed the soft shape of her bottom one last time before lifting his hands to her waist. He enjoyed the flare of her hips just past that indentation, almost fitting his hands around her.

Her breasts rose and fell rapidly against him as she breathed, blinking up at him as though trying to come out of a dream. "You're all hard again. This is embarrassing."

"It will be, if you don't stay here to protect me. Move away and they'll see what you've done to me." His delight in her, his awakening ex-wife, stunned him.

They'd stared at each other then, heat racing between them, zigzagging and skittering over them like electricity.

"I couldn't let you touch me that night. I felt too dirty."

"I know, but you're not. You're still an innocent and that's the problem," he'd said, aching for her.

Her hands had lightly smoothed his shoulders, shaping the powerful outline as if sizing him to her. She'd looked down to where he ached and then back up to meet his eyes. "We can't just be friends, can we?"

"I'm hoping for more," he'd answered, for nothing but the truth would do.

With a look that said she wasn't certain, she'd closed herself away again until her "We're here. Get out of the surrey."

With Gwyneth gone, the picnic table beneath the dappled moonlight in his mother's backyard had seemed the perfect slab upon which to place himself. His shredded hope of how the night would end, kissing Gwyneth, cuddling her, taunted him.

Then, in just the time it took her to get home and

return, the team of horses clip-clopped up Anna's drive-way. Lying on the old picnic table where he had been studying the stars, preparing a long, cold shower, Tanner appreciated the silvery moonlight on Gwyneth's long legs as she stepped onto the driveway. Clearly hunting him, she looked up at his old bedroom and then to the Boat Shop and from the set of her jaw and the tight fists at her side, he was to blame. She hurried across the lawn to him and within feet of him, she stopped and blinked. Tanner's whole body locked to the fast rise and fall of her breasts beneath the black dress, just those two gentle, moonlight-kissed mounds above the dress's modest square neckline. He let his eyes linger, rising up her throat to her flushed cheeks. In return, Gwyneth's fe-verish gaze remained locked on his body, which had hardened at her scent.

"You're at it again," she whispered huskily, as leaves whispered in the sultry summer night, and the slight breeze wrapped them in the scent of magnolia blossoms.

"Come lie here beside me, Gwyneth. Let me tell you about the stars and how a ship's course can be laid by them," he managed, for the pain in his lower body said that talking wasn't what he wanted, not after holding her close against him.

"On that old picnic table? The two of us?" Her voice trembled, softer than the midnight breeze stirring the leaves in the old maple tree above them.

"It's sturdy enough. I shored it up a bit, but it's lasted for years." *Just like my need for you. Trust me, Gwyn-eth, come lie by me.* "I'll tell you how the ocean rolls beneath a boat and you can tell me how it was, facing people without me, or Leather." He thanked old Leather then, the tough old man who kept the circling Romeos

away. He'd protected his daughter selfishly, but at least
she had that.

She shivered in the moonlight, and looked away to
the car passing on the country road nearby. In the distance, a cow lowed for her calf, and tree frogs croaked
and crickets chirped. "I know what you can do, how
much more you know than I... You don't go into the
house much, do you?"

"Not since I built the shop. My mother is still in the
house," he said simply, wanting to hold Gwyneth now,
not because of his desire, but because of another need—
that of a man needing to share his loneliness, to anchor
to the woman he'd always loved.

"I should have made her come with me. Life was too
hard here. I thought I'd get my boat business going better, then we'd take off for all the places she hadn't seen.
I wanted to sail her around the world. She wouldn't take
money—and those doilies of hers are dusty, needing
washing and starching."

He spread his fingers, too large for shaping ruffles into
sugar-starched doilies, even if he knew how. Callused
and scarred by years at sea and carpenter work, his hands
were broad in the palm and more suited to oars and
hammers. His mother's house was feminine and comfortable, yet he preferred the spartan furnishings of the
corner in his shop. "She ran a tight ship. I don't fit into
it as I did."

Who was he? *I've lost my mooring, sweetheart. I'm
adrift with a bad storm brewing...not a harbor or a safe
anchor in sight—except here, where I began and where
I came back to find peace. But the years at sea have put
a need in me, too. I want a home and children, and you
to cuddle amid life's storms.*

Gwyneth spoke softly. "She didn't want money. She

knew she had you and Kylie and Miranda. She had what she wanted. She'd loved a man, had his children and she was happy. She had more than most women could ever want.''

"She was still living on milk-and-egg money, vegetables, on midwifing and bottled vinegars and teas—she'd scrimped all of her life. She'd never been anywhere, seen anything." That old bitterness curled within him; he'd been too young to help much, but he had tried.

"You arrogant know-it-all." Gwyneth fisted his hair, with just enough pressure to emphasize her words. His hand shot out to shackle her wrist, giving her nothing. Her eyes flashed down at him, silver shards beneath the shadows of her lashes. This wasn't the timid girl he'd wanted as his wife, this was a woman who took matters into her own hands—except when they were her own deep, dark and terrifying secrets. "So that's what you've been brooding about. That's what is causing the dark, haunted look that just makes me want to— How arrogant you are, Tanner Zachariah Bennett. She had pride in what she did, supporting herself and tending to other people. Don't you dare look down at what she did."

He brought her wrist to his mouth, testing the fine inner skin with his thumb, tethering her close as he rose to stand in front of her. "Why did you come back tonight? 'Get out,' wasn't exactly a good-night kiss on a date's front porch."

"There you sat with Anna May's casserole on your lap and I—'' She clenched her lips, inhaled sharply and began again. "I had thinking to do, and it's difficult with you around or even feet from me. I feel this skittering up the back of my neck and you're there. I catch a scent, and I know it's you. The way you kiss, part sweet and tender and the other like you can barely keep from—oh, no, it doesn't scare me, not because I'm scared of you. But—oh, I'm getting all tangled up and that's why I wanted to be alone in the first place.... You knew I'd need you. That fine mess of knots won't let me untie that gorgeous hope chest and I'm not about to waste good rope by cutting through it. And I can't go asking the neighbors to come help me unload the heavy thing this time of night. I can't haul it around the countryside. You've got to come help me unload it.''

But he was set on his course, bound to know what ran through Gwyneth's mind now. ''Did you mind me touching you tonight? Holding you as we danced?''

She looked away again, and the tip of Tanner's finger turned her face back to him. ''Do you see them when I reach for you? In your fear, is it their faces over mine?''

''No. They were dirty. Leering. Drunk. You're you. Two separate images. You and them. Very different.'' Her words bit at the sweet night air, a slight tremble running through her body. Then she turned her back to him and protectively clasped her arms around herself.

''Don't shut me out, Gwyneth. Not this time,'' he said softly, wrapping his arms around her and rocking her. He lowered his cheek beside hers and relaxed a bit when she came softly back against him, trusting him.

Her hands turned with a jerk and her fingers locked onto his arms. ''Everything is gone, and you're trying to get it back to the same way it was,'' she whispered rawly, painfully. ''It's gone, Tanner. We were young, then. There are years between. Hard years for us both. You can't treat me like the innocent young bride-to-be that I was—I've changed.''

''Tell me how many times you've lain beside a man as you did on my cot. How many times you've let a man—*permitted a man*—to touch you like that, where you're dark and tight and sweet.'' Then because he knew Gwyneth would have to take her time coming to her own conclusions and forcing the issue could turn her away, Tanner caressed her bottom. He gave it a fond pat, before he managed somehow to walk to the surrey. ''Coming? You said you needed me?''

When he sat, holding the reins in his hands because his ego had taken enough of a battering that night and there were times that a man had to stand up for himself, Tanner saw that Gwyneth had not moved. Her hand was on her bottom, just where he had caressed. He couldn't help tease her.

''You have a fine bottom, Gwyneth. I was merely showing my appreciation.''

She tromped across the moonlit driveway and hefted herself easily up on the seat beside him. ''Patting me on the rump like a favorite cow or a dog,'' she muttered darkly.

''Not quite,'' he said carefully. ''But it's a shipshape piece of equipment.''

'''Equipment.' How would you like it if I—?'' She flushed suddenly and turned away.

''I'd like it fine. I'd like your hands on me anytime,'' Tanner said quietly, then flicked the reins.

Her stare sizzled at him as the horses' hooves clip-clopped toward her house. ''If you keep going at this rate, you'll have my hands on you and the result might be painful.''

''Go ahead, Gwynnie. Don't hold back. We'll see what happens,'' he invited with grin.

A half hour later, Gwyneth studied Tanner, lying on his back on her kitchen floor, his head and shoulders hidden beneath the kitchen sink. Looking very interested in his fix-up task, Penny and Rolf lay along one side of him, Gwyneth's battered toolbox opened on the other side and Tanner's dress shirt hung from the back of a chair.

As she stood over him, the black silky lace in her left fist burned, matching the brand of the pearl studs in her right fist. The pearls were sweet and classy, which she wasn't. The lacy short negligee and matching dance pants better suited a femme fatale, which she wasn't, either. Tanner's gifts in the hope chest were chosen for the message: he'd known women, made love to them and she wasn't up to par. "Exactly what are you doing?" she managed to ask between her teeth.

"Fixing this leak. I nearly broke my butt when I skidded across that old linoleum carrying your chest. You could have been hurt— Ouch!" He angled his head out to peer up at her and one hand rubbed his injured backside. "What was that kick for?"

"You can't give me things like this. That's what this is all about, isn't it? You're out for revenge. These are expensive, Tanner. And unsuitable for me. I'm better suited for an old T-shirt instead of a negligee."

"You've become a high-nosed hothead, sweetheart." Tanner's pleasant tone did not agree with the dark, savage gleam in his eyes. "And you're better suited for no clothing at all," he added as he came to his feet, towering over her in the tiny, neat kitchen.

His meaning scorched her, took away her breath, locked her bare feet to the worn linoleum floor, while her eyes locked to his bare, tanned chest. Sensing trouble, Penny and Rolf whined and Tanner jerked open the kitchen door, pointing outside. The obedient dogs reminded Gwyneth of how easily Tanner could control her emotions with one look—taking her body heat into simmering.

"I make my own choices now. I've run and fetched for one man all my life. I'd be a fool to take another. I'm my own woman," she stated shakily.

When he took a step toward her, she said, "We can't live together. Something will happen. You're not sweet, and apt to bully if I give you an inch."

"Nice inches," he murmured, black eyes sweeping down her body. "It's your call." He took another step as Gwyneth took one back. The dark hunger in his expression was enough to ignite her own and she wasn't certain how to handle the fire within her as he said, "It's malarky that women call the tune anyway. I should be calling on you and bringing you flowers and endearing my sweet self to you. It goes against the grain, sweetheart of mine, to let you choose the time and place—if ever—but so help me, I will."

"Tanner Bennett, you said you'd abide by—"

"So I did. But the wild, hot feel of you runs through me and—" He ran his fingers through his hair as though frustrated, peaking the shaggy black strands, and she noted the scars on his hands. Those marks were reminders that he'd been away for years, periodically visiting his mother. His wary look said he wasn't taking back his words, not to make her feel better.

She wanted to fling herself on him, to take his mouth and taste those dark, mysterious nuances. She wanted to run away from him, from what she was and wasn't. To shield her emotions, she looked at the worn pattern of the linoleum.

With a grim look, Tanner tore his shirt from the back of the chair and jammed his arms into the sleeves, not bothering to button it. "Is this what's bothering you? Or this?"

He reached slowly to curve his hand around her nape, his thumb pressing lightly to lift her chin as his mouth settled lightly upon hers. She searched his black eyes, so close to hers, the boy who had become a man and still could charm her breath away. Then his cheek, already rough with stubble, settled against her own and he whispered unevenly, "I've hungered for you a long time, Gwyneth, my love. It's been a lonely life without you."

Her fists clutched his lovely gifts between them, just over her rocketing heart. Then suddenly her arms flung around his shoulders, holding him tight. "Stay with me, Tanner, just for the night. Finish that night. Let me know how it could have been—"

For just a heartbeat, he drew away, his expression fierce and warring with another. He studied her and the sizzling vibrations between them hiked higher, trembling in the air, pounding at her—or was that her heart? Then with a reluctant groan, his mouth locked hungrily over hers, his hand cupping the back of her head as his other slid to hold her tightly against him, opened low on her spine. The hungry growl coming from him shot through her, locked deep within her, and there was no denying the surge of manhood that said he wanted her. He shook, his hand caressing a path down to her thigh to lift the hem of her dress and glide beneath it. His fingers eased gently around the elastic band of her briefs and then that incredible tightening bolted through her, causing her to cry out.

"Gwyneth…Gwyneth," he repeated roughly against her throat, his body trembling and hot against hers, his muscles taut around her. "You're too fast, too—"

He groaned again, taking her mouth, invading it with

his taste as he slowly drew down the zipper of her dress, easing her from it. Then his hard chest was against her again, skin burning skin, the scrap of lace torn away from her breasts. He gathered her closely against him, incredibly tender as if he didn't want to frighten her. As though he could withhold it no longer, a rough sound tore from him, his open hands splayed upon her hips caused her own keening sound, her body still contracting at the touch.

She wanted him close and tight and deep within her, making her forget the past, and empty, lonely future. She sought his roaming mouth, tried to capture it, and fought the feverish tide within her as Tanner's hands cupped her bottom and he began to carry her, kissing her, tormenting her all the while. He stopped in the hallway, groaned and leaned back against the wall, hitching her higher and easing her legs around his hips, which set her off again, that hard jean-covered nudge against her femininity. Gwyneth burned now, his open mouth branding her skin. "Don't let me go. Don't step away," she whispered desperately, fearing the return of her terror.

She had to keep him close, to protect them both, to see their journey finished. When Tanner eased her down upon the bed, she drew him over her, caught him with her legs and held him tight. She tethered him to her and fought the terror, keeping it away. Only when Tanner gently pried his gifts from her did she realize how badly she wanted to hold all of him, all that was him in her keeping. She opened her hands on his shoulders, caught his lovely mouth with hers and gloried in the freedom of his hunger.

Tanner moved suddenly, powerfully, tearing off his shirt and tossing it away. The movement startled her, that big body heavy upon her, with so much strength,

the muscles burning and shifting against her. But she
dug in her fingers, keeping him close. This was the man
she'd known all of her life, trusted enough to marry,
despite her father's objections. As a girl, she had been
intoxicated by one boyish look, one dark, searching look
that was meant only for her. As a woman, with scars in
her life, she wanted her due, to make love with Tanner.
She'd waited so long....

Then he was back with her, gathering her close into
his heat and safety, the muscles of his upper arms nudging her breasts, his heart racing against hers. There was
no time for thinking now, only flying....

A wisp of fear slithered through her and she flung it
away, digging in her fingers, locking herself to Tanner's
desire, and to her own. The exquisite pleasure of his
mouth on her breast caused her to cry out, her body
clenching as Tanner's shaking hands ran over her, locking on her bottom, lifting her to his desire, rocking
gently against her.

Then with Tanner's big body shaking over her, the
blunt pressure against her femininity and his mouth
pleasuring her breasts, the terror erupted, freezing her.
She pulled back into herself, then pushed free of the
terror as Tanner stilled, lifting his head to look down at
her. His face was hard, the muscles on his jaw defined.
His mouth locked into a grim line, a pulse throbbing in
his temple and another ran down his throat. She'd seen
that hard look of desire, of the male intent upon—

But this was Tanner...Tanner. He'd never hurt her.
She forced her body to relax beneath him, her heart racing from the passing terror. She stroked his hair, and
found his throat's hard, beating pulse with her lips. "It's
all right," she whispered, sensing his reluctance to push
her, though evidence of his need pressed close and ques-

tioning. "It's all right," she repeated, lifting her hips slightly, inviting him as her hands moved to his belt.

With a groan, he eased her hands from him and tore away his belt. She clenched her lids closed as he lifted slightly away, his hands moving between them. Then he was back, the pressure easing into her, slowly until she held him all, holding her breath and tightening again, rockets soaring, her body flying out of her control, and into Tanner's.

His rough sound went searing by her, and his thrust ignited her again and again. Suddenly Tanner was heavy upon her, all hers for now, resting his head on the pillow near hers, his heart pounding against her, his great body shaking violently. Gwyneth closed her eyes, smoothing his back, caring for him, because he seemed so vulnerable and uneasy while she was at utter peace. When she opened her eyes, it was to Tanner's fiercely bitter scowl as he eased from her.

He sat up abruptly, his back to her. In the dim light, his skin tightened and gleamed over taut muscles. He held his head in his hands as if he'd been defeated, then with a boiling curse stood to jerk up his slacks, fastening them on his way out of the house. The back door slammed, the sound tearing her heart apart. Amid the mussed bed, her body chilling from the loss of Tanner's, Gwyneth fought tears.

She had repulsed him, the man she'd waited for all her life. She hadn't known how to—

She curled into a ball on her side, pressed her hand against her mouth to muffle her cries, and the other pressed low on her stomach, that deep part that ached for him now. Amid her churning emotions, she realized that her terror of long ago was not there with Tanner, only the hunger, the seeking for completion. He hadn't wanted to linger with her, angry at himself, she thought, for having her. She felt like brittle ice, shattered and impossible to repair. She'd wanted him since that night, dreamed of him, and—she bit her lip to keep from crying out, forcing the cry deep down inside her as she had before.

A rough noise caught her, pinned her silently to the bed as Tanner's uneven deep voice echoed in the small, neat room. "Gwyneth, stop. Please don't cry. You're tearing me apart."

His weight behind her caused the bed to dip and she shrugged away his hand on her shoulder. His sharp intake of breath hissed through the room, and he eased the edge of the quilt over her nude body. She didn't want to look at him. She'd shown him her loneliness, her desperate need of him. She couldn't forgive him for making her see how wonderful it could have been.

"If I touch you, I'll want you again," he said roughly, not leaving her, though she flung his soothing hand aside.

"Want me?" Her boarded windows and her dogs and locks hadn't kept her safe, for she'd had needs to feed, the same as he—shocking, turbulent needs, as violent as a summer thunderstorm.

His voice was rough, dark and broody, falling heavily on her room, invading the safety she'd always known there. "I handled this poorly, Gwyneth. You caught me and winded me, and I wanted—"

"Experience?" she supplied bitterly.

"Snob," he said after the pounding silence of the room ate at her.

She flopped around toward him, careful to gather up the edge of the quilt against her. She scrubbed away her tears and glared at him. She'd been raised in the poorest way, dressed shabbily and Leather certainly wasn't class with his dirty, torn bib overalls and rough manners. *"What?"*

"You look down at me. I haven't jumped every woman I saw, you know. I've got some sense," he muttered darkly. "It's been years since I've been interested, if you have to know. I thought I could handle this, take it easy, get you used to me. I wasn't too certain that I could— Well, apparently I could and in record-rabbit time, not at all something I'm proud of. And you'll be wearing my bruises in the morning. Now that's a fine thing, isn't it. I'm no better than the—"

"Don't you dare say it. You're not taking the blame for this, Tanner. I chose what I wanted. I'm a thinking woman. You're not taking away any responsibility from me, and take back that 'snob' remark."

"You are and I'm not taking back anything. You're so high and mighty that you think you don't need anything. Everyone needs something, Gwyneth, including me. It burns me that I couldn't handle this better, that I didn't wait—"

She fisted the quilt, getting angry with him now. "Burns you?"

He scrubbed his open hands over his face. "You're repeating everything I say. I had other plans, that's all. The long, slow, loving kind."

Gwyneth's temper hitched up into danger. She'd jumped him, laid him out and had him. Another woman would have played more softly into his arms and kept him close, stirring him again. "Other plans with whom?"

Then because anger drove her on, she said tightly, "There's the door. I'm certain there are plenty of women out there—"

"There aren't. I tried," he stated curtly. Over the width of his bare, gleaming shoulder, Tanner's expression was that of disgust. "We skipped the friendship-relationship foundation part and went right for the basics. All you had to do was touch me and I—"

He frowned at her as she waited for each word, turning it like a bright new coin, and wondering how she could affect him so, and when would be the next time, and why couldn't he control himself, and why—?

Tanner snorted roughly, placed a big hand on her face and pushed her lightly back onto the pillow. "Don't think so hard. I can just see the wheels going round. We just bypassed some essentials, that's all. And now that I've had a taste of you—"

"That's right, you did taste me, didn't you? It seems only fair—" She eyed his powerful shoulders and the slow smile upon his lips. He'd taste delicious, of course—

He chuckled at her openly curious expression, brought her hand to his lips, kissing the back. "See you tomorrow."

In the silence after Tanner left her room, quietly closing the door behind him, Gwyneth tried to adjust to his fierce taking, her claiming of him, the power she had over him, and the softness he made her feel, as though he needed her to be a part of him.

She leaped out of bed, paused and found his shirt lying on the floor. Picking it up, she hurriedly put it on, catching his scent, needing to see him safely cross the field between their homes. She jerked open the back door and before her sight adjusted to the starlit night, ran into Tanner's broad, hard back.

Her instincts told her to capture him, to drag him back into her keeping, and she realized her arms tightly closed around his waist. It was a wrestler's hold, her hands locked on her wrists. She had little time for thinking or tenderness, but meanwhile, he wasn't leaving her. His hands closed on her arms, keeping her tight against his back. He rolled his back against her breasts as though luxuriating in the feel of her and then stood silent, staring at Anna's house in the distance.

Gwyneth held him tighter, for she couldn't let him go to the empty house where haunting, loving memories could leap upon him. She couldn't let him go to that cold building, lie on that narrow cot. She placed her cheek against his strong back, absorbing the loneliness within him. "Stay with me," she whispered and forgave herself the light kiss she had to place on his back.

She'd been taught not to hug or kiss, that such things were silly and weak. But in defiance of Leather, she kissed Tanner's bare back again and her arms lifted as he breathed slowly, deeply and he relaxed against her. He placed her hand over his heart and breathed quietly, as though he were just exactly where he wanted to be. "I'll be in later," he said in the easy tone a husband would tell a wife.

He could have been saying that same thing, all those years between. Against his back, she closed her eyes, careless of the tear that squeezed onto his skin—

"Leave me, honey," Tanner murmured, his body suddenly taut, hard muscles flexing against her cheek.

Minutes later, fresh from her shower, Gwyneth lay listening to the noises of a man settling a house, talking quietly to her dogs, turning off the lights, and taking his shower. She held the collar of his dress shirt up close to her cheek, inhaling his masculine, dark scent amid scents of soap and shaving cream with a slight bite of lime. She stretched out in bed, wearing his shirt and sizing his larger body to hers. She looked at the ceiling and saw his face, honed by desire—desire for her. In her scramble for that shocking fulfilment, she'd known how strong he was. His muscles had shifted over her, his powerful thighs pressed against hers, locking the fit. Yet he'd held himself back, until that last shuddering groan as if he didn't want to give himself and couldn't help ending the race she'd begun so wildly—

When he left the bathroom, her throat went dry, her nerves skittering and alert— If he came to her, she couldn't trust herself. She hadn't exactly given him the full measure of what a woman could give a man.

Then she heard the bed creak in Leather's room.

It was hours before she slept, because she knew that Tanner was carefully guarding his emotions, just as she feared hers. She'd hurt him terribly once, and she could again. Gwyneth frowned, suddenly caught by a whirlwind of images of Tanner poised over her, his expression fierce. Her body was restless, aching and tender *and she wanted him again.* She flopped over on her side, smoothed the pillowcase where his head had rested, the dark mysterious scent of him curling around her. If she had more experience, she might go into his room…

She thrashed to her other side, the bed creaking beneath her. She hadn't controlled herself; she'd probably leap upon him and unman him, though she doubted that—there was so much of Tanner all over.…

She groaned shakily, smoothing her tender body, and aching for his hands on her breasts, his mouth tugging erotically at her— She squirmed restlessly in her bed, the springs creaked, and far away the old owl hooted in the night.

She flopped again, wanting the man in the next room. Her pride kept her from moving and Tanner's deep chuckle was soft and wicked and gave her little reason to sleep.

Seven

Men have to have their due, it seems, a warlord
bred into them at birth. Once they get their hackles up, it's up to us to soothe them. Once a
woman understands that a man's needs go deeper
than his swaggering and play, she's on an easier
road. It's a courtly thing they need, seeing after
us. But here in Freedom Valley, the woman does
the choosing and asking, if she's set upon the
man. Sometimes it's best to let them have their
way and in doing so, have our own needs met.

—Anna Bennett

Gwyneth's small kitchen mirror held proof of Tanner's
sleepless night. The man looked haunted, shadows under
his eyes, a morning beard latched to his set jaw, and a
wary look in his eyes. Sleep wasn't an activity he could

sink into, with Gwyneth crying out, her terror scurrying through the shadowy house.

If he would have gone to her, held her as he needed to, he would have frightened her more.

Tanner wrapped his hand around the steaming mug of coffee, and grimly poured a warming bit more from the old tin pot he'd found in the cabinet. He ran his thumb over the mug's rim, noting the old chip. He felt as worn, and replaced the pot to a folded, well-washed tea towel. Rubbing the back of his stiff neck didn't help the stormy mood inside him. The old stuffed chair in her bedroom had offered little comfort as he watched Gwyneth toss and turn; he'd wished he'd had those men within his hands.

And what of him? Was he so different? He hadn't bothered to take off his slacks, hurrying on with her. *He'd had her with his clothes around his ankles.* That image didn't do much for his ego, or his pride. He climbed the masts of sailing ships in high storms, and yet he couldn't control the hunger snaking through him, for this woman.

He glanced at the freshly washed eggs in the wire basket draining in the chipped sink that should have been replaced long ago. Gathering them and bringing the cows back to Gwyneth's to milk had kept him busy for a time while she slept.

So much for control. So much for discovering what-ever ran between them, and separating it from the past, sifting through truth and— He'd wanted more. He'd wanted to hold her gently, to cuddle her.

He'd stay this morning to face her, to take his share of guilt, and try to start a more tender...

Tender? He'd taken what he could get and leaped into

the fire with her when he should have known better, and given her more.

She'd awaken soon, her nightmares exhausting her. He wanted to be here, in her home, to let her know he wouldn't have her and then be off without apologizing. He studied the kitchen, the steady drip of the faucet needing a new washer. Leather hadn't given his daughter much for comfort. The home was barren, the bathroom ceiling proof that the roof needing more than a patching. Neat, scrubbed-clean and shabby, the counters needed to be replaced and the cabinet doors hung akilter, the soft pine wood too cheap and damaged to save.

He wanted more for her; he wanted to take care of her, provide for her, and knew that her pride wouldn't stand for his help.

Tanner scrubbed his hands over his face and settled for staring at his feet, bare upon the worn yellow linoleum. There would be penalties for leaping into his hunger, and he didn't like the heavy fear clawing at him that Gwyneth couldn't bear to look at him this morning. He rose impatiently to his feet and leaned back against the counter, crossing his arms and praying that she'd talk to him; he'd stay, and take what came.

He wasn't prepared for what did come, the drowsy, mussed woman padding into the kitchen, reaching out a hand to snag his mug of coffee and the other to grab a soda biscuit he'd made, munching on it as she walked toward her studio. Though she hadn't noticed him in the shadows, Tanner's heart kicked into gear and roared in his ears. The impulse to take her in his arms and carry her back to bed rode roughly through him, yet he knew that he needed more—he needed her trust, not just her body.

Meanwhile, his body's ache for Gwyneth was too ob-

vious. The button of his too-big shirt had come open,
revealing the slope of her breast, and when she turned,
the light fabric had clung to her curved bottom, the hem
enticing at midthigh. The slender legs that slid into bare
feet jolted him, because his body reacted, remembering
how strong she'd been holding him to her, reaching for
him…

Tanner ran his shaking hand down his jaw. The sight
of her in his shirt had set him off again, just that tantalizing glimpse of thigh before her long legs ran on—
fascinated and pleasured him.

Still half-asleep, Gwyneth sipped the coffee she must
have made earlier, when she really preferred a good peppermint tea in the morning. At times, she'd wake early,
doing bills on the kitchen table, and making coffee, more
for the delicious scent than the taste. She must have
made the biscuits, too, though they tasted better than the
tinned, refrigerator kind, melting in her mouth. She inhaled slowly, feeling too tired, but tired was normal for
her. The heavy, sated feeling was new and warm and
comfortable. She hadn't come into her studio to work,
but to check the pots she'd made the day before to see
if they were leather-hard. If they were ready, she'd plan
on trimming them in the late hours, after hauling the
calves to market and—

She yawned, wondering why the rooster wasn't crowing; she must have let Penny and Rolf outside earlier,
and they'd be chasing the high-stepping, fine-feathered
monster if he made too much noise, taunting them. She
slid into a comfortable old wood chair, and rested her
crossed legs on another.

A sound at the studio door brought her fully awake,
and Tanner, leaning against the wall, studied her. His

crossed arms, the gleam of bare hard muscles did little to stop the shaking of her hand.

"Good morning," he said in an intimate tone that took her scrambling back into the night, when he'd lain over her, his voice dark and heady and magical against her skin, heating her. Awake now, she recognized the cause of her slightly aching body. The hard tug deep within her caused her to tremble, a hot drop of coffee sloshing onto her thigh, onto the dress shirt she'd worn to keep him close.

Dressed only in his slacks, a tea towel slung over his broad shoulder, and his feet bare upon the old boards of her studio floor, Tanner held another cup of coffee in one hand. He looked comfortable as a man in his own home.

She could handle this: The Morning After. She could, she told herself again as those black sultry eyes drifted over her from her bare feet up the length of her legs and higher until they boldly, hotly met her own stare, drying her throat and thumping her heart into overdrive.

"So now we know. Do you hurt?" he murmured grimly in the manner of a man who would have his due and settle what ran between them, rather than to shove it back into the night.

She nodded, unable to speak, the biscuit crumbling in her grip. She wouldn't deny that she'd wanted him; she wouldn't say she was sorry for her inexperience. Life had come hard to her, and she'd taken that joy, clasping it close within her heart. She glared at him, daring him to say something to set her off, waiting—

"I asked you if you hurt." He wasn't leaving the intimacy she'd wanted to crawl back into.

"It's new, that's all, no more than an ache."

"Maybe you should see a doctor. To see if—you were

so tight, Gwyneth. I could have hurt you." His voice was uneven, rough with emotion.

"I'm not letting—" she began, looking away as her assault drifted in the musty air between them. "I'm fine."

The curling of his hand into a fist told her that rage still flowed through him, the need to make the men pay. "You're not letting a man touch you, I know. And then there was me. Why?"

"For old times' sake?" she asked blithely, uneasy with the intimacy. Then because she could match him now, she locked her eyes with his. "I wanted you. You wanted me."

"You don't owe me anything but the truth." A big man, Tanner filled her shadowy, small, cluttered studio as he moved toward her. She caught the scent of soap and his dark mysterious essence amid the earth scents of clay. She would have pulled her feet away from their place on the chair, but instead, he scooped a hand beneath her ankles. He lifted them until he sat, and then resettled her feet upon his lap. One hand smoothed her legs as he sipped his coffee. Tanner's mood wasn't as easy flowing as his words, for one dark searing look sent electricity skittering over her body. "So this is where you find comfort, is it?"

"Like you, when you build your boats." She wasn't explaining her dreary life, how this was her only pleasure and the pride that it allowed her to pay her bills. Here amid the musty earth scents of clay, she found some small bit of peace. She wouldn't explain why she wore his shirt, though she tried to gather it more closely around the legs he was studying, his hand smoothing higher. "I made this. It's mine. I built it—for me."

Just as she had taken last night, out of greed that Tanner had jerked to life—

He smoothed her foot, the soft intimacy more frightening. "So here we are," he murmured, as if placing young Gwyneth and Tanner in another time, away from the man and woman who had joined in a thunderbolt of passion the night before.

"I expected you'd be gone." She'd been disappointing, she knew. Her body had jolted out of control, and she hadn't time for the slow stroking and petting she'd seen actresses do in movies.

Anger leaped from him, searing her, then it was quickly shielded. "You think so little of me. You think that's all I want. Maybe I want more."

The brooding statement shocked her, the next speared into her heart. "I want romance, Gwyneth-mine. I want to hold and cuddle and take care of you. I want us to share more than what happened last night, and yet I want that, too."

"I had you, cold and flat—" She flushed and turned away, still shocked by the hunger that had risen out of her last night. It still simmered within her now and she locked her body against the need.

His lifted black brow mocked her. "This isn't a winner-takes-all situation and I'm hoping for equal opportunity. I wouldn't exactly call it cold, honey. I just wasn't ready for the fireworks. You caught me by surprise. I was up to bat too quickly and I'm not proud of having you with my pants around my ankles."

"You were all there—" she protested in her defense, because she wasn't apologizing for anything. She had enough of old Leather in her to meet the consequences of what she'd done, but enough to hold up for herself, too.

"That I was, all engines humming. But you ignite too quickly. You didn't give me a chance to show off my finer points."

She snorted at that, for it was a wicked gleam that Tanner slid up her legs and higher, coming to rest on the dark nubs beneath his dress shirt. Then he leaned over to give her a kiss that was more friendly than sensual. She kissed him back, and amid the shadowy, musty clay scents, she found herself blushing and wanting him.

"Are you going to court me, Gwyneth?" he asked softly. "Because if you're not, we'd better do some fast thinking as to why that surrey wasn't returned last night. I unhitched the horses last night, but that fancy rig makes a real statement out by your barn. And if Sadie McGinnis calls—yes, I did have a tiny bit of sense left at the last minute, enough to use protection."

The rest of the biscuit crumbled within her shaking fist, the bits dropping onto the rough planks of her flooring. The Women's Council would know Tanner spent the night, and they would be visiting to see if he'd moved in and was taking proper care of her. Minutes ticked away as she stared at Tanner, whom she could claim or send home. "You could stay here, and that would make you a bit more comfortable than in Anna's house, or in that huge shop. You keep the doors open and the birds will be roosting in the rafters—"

"I'd definitely be more comfortable here," he agreed seriously and she didn't trust the wicked gleam in his eyes.

"We'll fight. I like to have my own way and I'm not used to waking up in the morning to a cold, hard toilet with a lifted seat," she said.

He nodded slowly. "Uh-huh. I'll try to be considerate."

"You'll have to make yourself comfortable. I don't have time to coddle you. If you shame me in front of the Women's Council, of which I am a member, I'll kill you. We're doing a good job and have for years and I won't have that marred by you or the Bachelor Club."

"I'll be perfect," he purred with a look that said he wouldn't be. "But, Gwyneth, you haven't asked me for a date. Isn't that one of the Rules for Bride Courting?"

"I'll think about it, but you're not pushing me," she said carefully, while she tried to ignore the pleasure his hands gave her feet.

"While you're thinking about it, why don't you think about this?" he asked, leaning closer to give her a dazzling, seeking kiss that sent her head spinning.

While she reeled from that heady kiss, tasting his desire, she opened her eyes to Tanner's close inspection. "Why haven't you made the lamps you want?" he asked.

She blinked, trying to place her body and mind together. "They take time. I know I have ready-made sales with mugs and soup bowls. If I spent time with a lamp, matching an upper and lower bowl, matching the diameters, it would take hours more and the risk of loss in the kiln is too great. There are too many things that can go wrong and could be easily ruined, the time wasted."

His fingers, wrapped around hers, tightened. "You're saying you don't take chances."

"I can't." She knew they were talking on two levels now, a skill that Tanner knew and she had yet to learn.

"It's called 'trust,'" he said quietly. "Trust in yourself. Trust in me. It will work out, one way or the other."

He could have been a seaman coming home, Gwyneth thought as Tanner walked across the field from Anna's.

With his heavy duffel bag slung across his shoulder, and dressed in a white T-shirt and jeans, Tanner walked across the sunset playing in the field like a man who knew what he wanted and where he was going. Just the sight of him, all broad shouldered, his black shaggy waves lifted a bit by the late July breeze, that earring gleaming in his ear, lifted her heart and made it dance.

While Rolf and Penny ran eagerly toward him, Gwyneth eased back into the shadows of the barn, where she'd just put away the shovel from cleaning the chicken house. She couldn't run to him, leap on him and bear him to the ground as she wanted; pride and caution held her back. She smelled like cow and work, not the woman who could keep Tanner close and interested. The horror of her need last night ran through her again, when she'd opened her heart and her body from its safe moorings and taken him desperately. She covered her hot face with her hands. She hadn't seen him all day, and prayed he'd changed his mind. She could live with gossip....

She opened the two fingers covering her eyes and saw him heft the heavy duffel bag onto his other shoulder. As he strode across the field, she eased farther back into the shadows.

How could she trust herself? Through the distance his body called to hers, that mouth and wicked grin— She could feel the need rumbling in her like a volcano about to burst.

She looked around the corner as Mel Rosenstein's Lumberyard truck pulled alongside her house. Tanner greeted Mel, opened the house, entered and came out without his duffel bag.

Dahlia Greer's and Elke Blake's vans pulled off the

road and stopped behind Mel's truck. The Committee for the Welfare of Brides piled out of the vans.

Gwyneth closed her eyes and shook her head. She'd been in those vans on occasions like this. She'd asked questions, all in good fun, of the couple intending to say their vows. "Gwyneth, dear," Fidelity Moore called in her high, quivery voice. "Tanner says you're hiding in the barn. That won't do. Come along now. We've got questions."

She could have killed Tanner as he stood with his hands on his hips, grinning at her. "I'm awfully busy, Fidelity. Could we do this another time?"

"You returned the surrey a little late this morning, dear. There are matters to be discussed. We need to know how you feel and to insure that you have proper care, that is, if you wish to go along with the customs of Freedom Valley. You're free not to, of course, just as you did before. But Tanner has said he wants marriage and since you're already to this point, living together, it seems, the Committee feels you need this inspection. Since there is no one else to do so, the Founding Mothers would have wanted us to be very careful with a lovely, sweet girl like you. Anna would want this, too, because that's how it's always been in her family."

Gwyneth groaned, wiped her dirty hands on her cutoff jeans and knew she smelled like the hard work she'd been doing all day to keep her mind off Tanner. Taking a deep, steadying breath, she forced herself out of the barn and walked to the ladies and Tanner.

Dahlia Greer, an experienced woman who knew men and loved each and every one, had a very knowing and wicked grin. She appreciated good-looking men, which was clear from the way she was eyeing Tanner as he and Mel began unloading the lumber truck. "Oh, my," she sighed as Tanner hefted the two-by-fours on his shoulder and the muscles of his arms surged in the dying sun. "No wonder she jumped him."

"Is that what he told you?" Gwyneth asked tightly, ready to defend herself, even if it was the truth. She'd had him, tugged him over her and captured him and gave his first resistance not a second thought.

"He said you'd been apart long enough and he wanted to take care of you. But when that man comes calling, a woman would be a fool not to grab him," Dahlia answered easily.

Mary Lou Walters and Jasmine Thatcher and Ava Sanders all carried boxes. "Tanner didn't think it was right for him to give you these, though I'm certain that there are things he wants to give you of Anna's. These are all Anna's work, made for her son's home, and since he made you a hope chest, it would be a lovely place to keep them, until you're truly married," Mary Lou said. "We'll just take them in the house. I want to see the lovely hope chest he made you. His father did such lovely work."

"This winter, after he has your house in good shape and his business going well, he's going to repair our antique furniture at no cost, and the Women's Council may have a charity boating day next year. We're going to dress in elegant 1880's dresses and use parasols, and the perfect Saturday will be my birthday. I'll be ninety-one, you know," Fidelity exclaimed, her blue eyes alight. She leaned closer to Gwyneth and whispered in an aside, "His mother would have a fit at the way he tends her herbal beds and the herbs are going to waste. Maybe you could help him? You can't just let him do all the running, dear. Fish get off the hook, if the line isn't tended, you know," she advised. "Do your part, too. Or the Committee can't be responsible."

Gwyneth inhaled sharply as Tanner and Mel muscled a new toilet into her house, and later a kitchen sink. She closed her eyes as bundles of shingles were stacked up against her house, and the men began unloading the lumber, working their way back to two huge crates.

"A new stove with all sorts of gizmos, buttons up high and safe from any little hands that might come along," Elke, the mother of eight children, said. "He likes to cook. He said it will take a while to redo the kitchen counters so he can add a dishwasher."

"A new refrigerator, too. Tanner said he'd have to build an addition before adding the new washer and dryer. He doesn't want you lugging your laundry down to Suds Your Own, though Antoinette will be sorry to lose your business."

Fidelity tapped her cane on the boards. "Good man. Wants you to have an easier life. What do you have to say for yourself, Gwyneth Smith Bennett?"

"I could—" Kill him, Gwyneth finished silently. Take his thick neck and wring it… She couldn't afford the mountain of lumber and shingles and appliances on Mel's truck, never, ever. Tanner was shaming her, making her life look shabby and poor, and she'd worked too hard to— "He's moved in. We'll see," she managed to say finally.

"That's his father's rocking chair. Our boy is a family man," Lila Rivers said quietly as Tanner carried the chair into Gwyneth's front door.

In a moment, he leaned out of the kitchen door. "Ladies, I've made some lemonade. Can I serve it out here?"

"Such a lovely boy Anna raised," Fidelity crooned.

"We can do without the lemonade. It's late July and canning and gardening time, you know. We'll ask a few questions as is the custom and then we'll be on our way. Come out here, son. We need to see you together, you and Gwyneth. She seems a little stricken now, but then with all this happening and her prince back to stay, what woman wouldn't be?"

She sniffed delicately in Gwyneth's direction, obviously noting the eau de chicken house. "Dear, you always used to be so tidy. Don't let yourself go, now that you've got Tanner's attention again. He's such a prince."

Tanner came to stand beside Gwyneth, ignoring the sturdy keep-away nudge of her elbow. His charming smile did not reach his eyes, and the look he shot down at her was wary. He wrapped his arm around her waist too firmly, a warning. "We're ready. Ask away. Next time you come around, I hope it will be for our open house."

"No need for questions. She's glowing and obviously quite happy. I think it's marvelous that the Bachelor Club is helping you set up housekeeping. Tanner said they're eager to help," Sadie stated. "It will keep those rapscallions out of trouble for a time, and maybe they can learn something from a man with honest intentions. Now let's go help Gwyneth pack Anna's things into her hope chest. I'm certain she'll want them safe with all the sawdust that's certain to be blowing around."

She sniffed delicately in Gwyneth's direction. "We'll wait, of course, if you want to shower."

An hour later, the ladies departed and Gwyneth, drained and furious, flung herself facedown on her bed. She dug her fingers into the quilt that Anna had made her long ago, her life in pieces without a circle design or neat stitches to hold her together. She wasn't used to anger for one thing; Tanner knew how to scrape away all the layers she'd built up through the years and tear at the hard-won foundations of her life. Tanner taking a shower in the bathroom did little to calm her.

When the water stopped and the bathroom door closed, she flipped over on her back, prepared to launch herself at him. The sight of Tanner leaning against the doorjamb, his arms crossed, and wearing nothing but a clinging, worn towel around his hips, stopped all thought. Beads of water danced on his tanned shoulders and gleamed in the wedge of dark hair on his chest.

"Problems?" he invited tightly, clearly out to tear her from her stormy silence. She gave him that—Tanner never ran from trouble and she was going to give him plenty.

"It's just too much," she muttered, finally finding the words. Gwyneth failed in her attempt to drag her eyes from his body and wanted to place her fingertip just there, in that exciting indentation in his flat, ridged stomach and to trace lower—

"Yes, it is," he agreed grimly. "We didn't take the usual course, going at each other last night before we understood what ran between us. But here we are, ready or not. They jumped me at the shop, and I had to come up with something that didn't make me look like I was living off you. Think of this as a gift. Carpentry is what I know. I want to give you gifts. Is that such a bad thing?"

"You've got your boats to build, even if I could repay you for the supplies and I won't take charity."

"A man likes to do for his woman, no matter what the customs are, Gwynnie. It goes against my pride, that you're making more of it than it is."

"I hate when you call me 'Gwynnie,' like I'm six—"

"You're acting like it now." Tanner's smoothly shaven jaw locked, skin gleaming over taut muscles. His eyes narrowed, slashing at her, the cords on his throat taut with anger. "You think I would have you and walk away? You think last night didn't mean anything to me? You think I'd live off you, and not do my share? What I know how to do best—work with my hands—that I'd keep that from you? Do you think so little of me?"

"Take it back," she whispered, shaking now. She'd hurt him, she knew, but pride kept her going. "Take all of it back."

"Last night?" he rapped at her, his smile cold. They stared at each other, each seasoned by the years between, each with individual terms. Then Tanner tore away the towel, hurled it onto a battered chair and stalked away from her, leaving her with the sight of an anger-taut, well-muscled back. "I'm going to the shop," he said harshly. "It's safer there, and like you said, I've got boats to build."

Moments later, the soft click of the door behind him shattered her heart.

Eight

Pride can keep a man and a woman apart. Sometimes, it's best left in the slop bucket, so the tender web of healing can begin, the understanding of what was said and what that look meant, and all the rest. While you're filling the slop bucket, toss in bitterness and revenge. They take you nowhere, but to pain. Replace what you have tossed away with trust and love.

—Anna Bennett

She'd never gone after a man, but she'd wounded Tanner's pride. *For Anna, I'll try to be more gentle,* Gwyneth thought, and tossed away the lie. She needed Tanner in a softer way, for herself, to keep him safe and close, though she didn't know the whys just yet. At the shop's side door, just feet from Anna's backyard and the big

CAIT LONDON   153

magnolia tree, Gwyneth placed her fingertips over her
swollen eyes. The grit of crying still lodged there, despite her attempts to soothe it with a cold washcloth.
Karolina Jones had been too shrewd in her assessment,
her voice excited across the telephone lines—"You
what? You got a man and lost him all in the same day?
It's only seven o'clock at night. You work fast, girl."

Karolina had called an hour after Tanner had gone.
Hoping he'd call, Gwyneth had snatched the telephone
from its cradle, and answered before clearing the telling
sobs from her throat. Onto a good mystery, Karolina
leaped straight into the killer conclusion— "So he's not
there. He's working at the shop. You returned the surrey
this morning, looking all hot and flustered, according to
Mr. Peters," she said, switching to her click-click offi-
cial manner. "The bottom line is that things are not good
between you and Mr. Bennett in only a matter of hours.
According to Fidelity—Mrs. Alfonso Moore—the Committee was more than satisfied with Mr. Bennett's attempt at presenting his husband candidacy. On the other
hand, you smelled like chicken doo. Something hap-
p   d after the ladies left. He's holed up. Men do that
cave withdrawal thing when they're upset. They're delicate creatures, despite the muscles, and have to be handled with care. Tell me all... I won't divulge an in-
former's name to Serefina Malagay. She's getting a help
for the lovelorn column going at the paper. Is he coming
home tonight or not?"

While Gwyneth refused to answer Karolina's questions, her pen scratching in the background, she wasn't
certain about Tanner. What the ladies thought didn't
matter; she'd faced gossip before.

She'd hurt him again. He'd given her a gift of himself,
and dug deep in her own pride, she'd hurled it in his

face. She wrapped her fingers around the big brass knob and took a steadying breath before opening the door. Soothing a male's rumpled hackles was a skill she'd never tried, and his cool stare down her T-shirt and jeans gave her little comfort.

She'd known him all her life. He'd fixed her broken wagon when Leather didn't have time. Tanner had held her close and safe, and now the distance between them stretched into galaxies. He turned back to his work, ignoring her, hurting her.

She wanted to comfort him, to let him know that she cared, but layers of pride and Leather's harshness held her still.

She couldn't let him hate her, not a second time. She had to touch him, hold him, and— Tanner's broad back looked forbidding. Trembling, hesitant and fearing he would turn her away, Gwyneth straightened her shoulders and walked toward him.

He tensed, his breath sucking in, tightening those taut muscles of his stomach, as she slid her arms around his body. She leaned against him, simply rested there, anchored to his safety and warmth and the gentle, good man she knew he was. He stood very still as she held him, her cheek against his back, his heart skipping rapidly beneath her palm.

He turned slowly within her arms, holding them tight with his hands, until he looked down at her. The emotion charging him leaped to her, dived in and wrapped around her heart. She stood on tiptoe to kiss him, and then his arms were around her, his mouth opening on hers in a hunger that told her what she needed to know. He breathed roughly against her skin, holding her close, speaking unevenly. He kissed each dimple and tasted her lips. ''Witch. Pretty little, enticing, hot-blooded witch.

How am I going to hold my own against you? You can't always have your way, though right now, I'm not certain of that."

"Does it mean so much to you, fixing the house?"

"Yes," he whispered roughly, holding her tighter. "It does. It's inside me, to make a home. I knew how you'd take it, but there it was, the chance to be with you and so I took it."

"It goes down hard. I promised myself I wouldn't need anyone," she said, looking up into Tanner's searching, soft, dark eyes. She'd bend her stiff-necked pride for him, try to learn give-and-take.

"If we'd had more time— Do you need me, sweetheart?"

His pride needed mending, and terms would have to be set, she knew. She couldn't answer, but latched her arms around his shoulders and held him tight, kissing him with all the hunger in her. Tanner's arms went around her waist, lifting her higher to his lips. "You thought you'd come get me, have me and drag me back to your lair, is that right?" he asked between the tiny, teasing kisses across her mouth, her cheeks, her nose and eyes.

"Yep. That's about it." She drifted above the floor, certain that a silly telling smile was pasted on her face.

He kissed her again, one of those long, soul-sucking, heavenly kisses that caused her fingers to dig into his shoulders. Then he said, "Well, it's a good try, but I'm wanting romance, not wham-bam...though at times—"

He drew an unsteady breath and eased her away. His cocky look reminded her of when he was playing ball and caught a chancy one to win the game. "We'll fight. Redoing a house costs in more ways than one, but I'll

always come home. Go on now...let me clean this
away.''

Unsteady in her emotions, but eased, Gwyneth wan-
dered around his shop. A man who carried his father's
craft within him, though he could do whatever he
wanted, Tanner's tools were neatly arranged, and very
clean. Some were obviously treasured, set apart from the
rest. On his desk, tossed carelessly aside, she found a
well-worn chain of silver, heavy-duty; it was made for
a man, an ivory pendant attached to it. Her image was
carved in scrimshaw, the way she'd looked as a girl, her
long hair freed of braids and blowing in the wind—

When Tanner walked to her, she gripped the pendant
in her fist, her heart racing away without her. ''Why?''

He smoothed her cheek with his fingertips and the
drift of his eyes over her face was quiet and certain.
''Because the need of you never stopped, no matter
where I went or what I did. You were always a part of
me.''

His bitter words, hurled years ago, churned within her.
''I thought you hated me, that you were out for revenge.''

''I did for a time. Did you think that I'd had the
women of the world?'' he asked, teasing her.

She looked up into the humor flirting around his face,
and found her own smile on her lips. ''How about dinner, at the café? Today is Willa's cherry pie day, and
the blue plate specials are all you can eat.''

''Who's buying?'' he asked, noting that she liked to
pay her bills and took little from anyone.

''You are,'' she said after hesitating, dealing with the
past and trying new steps, and because she intended to
allow him his pride, too. Tanner was an old-fashioned
male, deep down, and he had to be tended carefully.

*   *   *

"Get away. I'm making progress with the Women's Council. You'll contaminate me and take me back to the Cull bin. Tomorrow is Saturday. Be at the house around four in the morning," Tanner said easily to Fletch and York as they came to sit beside him. A women's summer ball game drew men like flies, all that sweaty, soft female flesh quivering beneath the floodlights. Despite the late July heat, the bleachers were full. Husbands tended children while mothers played on the field, cheering for them. Boys came to watch Freddie—Fredricka Olendorf—because of her statuesque measurements, and the single men enjoyed the other females playing on the field, too.

"When the food runs out at Gwyneth's, I'm gone," Fletch said. "The things a guy does for an old friend."

"The faster the house is remodeled, the sooner you'll be selling and fixing those cute little outboard motors for my boats," Tanner returned.

"I like to make motors purr," Fletch murmured, eyeing Fredricka's voluptuous body.

The night after they'd parked by the lake, Tanner wasn't letting anything spoil his winning streak. Gwyneth, prettily mussed and lacking her bra from their session at the lake, had studied him at her bedroom door. He could feel the hot, wild hunger in her, a match to his own, but he had set his course to smooth the trouble between them. Gwyneth believed he was just passing through, settling his grief and his pride, but he intended to stay a lifetime. If he came into her bed, he wouldn't be leaving, and there were too many problems yet to go. She'd flinched when he'd reached to pluck a straw from her hair, and that set him in a surly, frustrated mood; he cursed the men who had created her fear.

She'd forgotten him this morning, drowsily accepting a mug of tea from him as she padded by on her way to her studio. Moments later, she'd come out to sniff at his waffles and ate two before blinking up at him, her tongue licking at the syrup on her lip. He'd forced himself away from that vision, because if he hadn't, they'd have spent the day—

She forgot to kiss him as she walked out the door. Despite his intentions to let her choose her time, Tanner had snagged her back to him and had filled his need, leaving them both shaking and hot and staring at each other. Then he'd hiked off to the shop, taking what little pride he could manage with him.

Fletch dug into his small picnic cooler and handed Tanner a cold cola. "Take that and run, ye who wants out of the Cull pit."

The good-natured taunt flicked Tanner's defiance, and he boldly ignored Sadie McGinnis's hard, condemning stare, settling back on the bleacher to watch Gwyneth play first base. After all, there were advantages of sitting just where he was, on the wooden bleachers directly behind first base. When she crouched, leaning forward, hands on knees and waiting for the pitch—

"I'm in a fragile mood," he muttered as Fredricka rounded the bases on a home run and the male eyes swung to her. Then Gwyneth turned to him, narrowing her gaze to see if he'd looked at Fredricka, too. He blew her a kiss and delighted in the way she noted the other gaping males tracing Fredricka.

"Men get that way, when they're going through this," Fletch was saying. "The whole thing is unnatural. Men cooking and pulling equal duty in the house. Bet you've got a pot roast on right now, for after the game—"

Fletch stopped talking as he watched Fredricka joyously bounce up and down after trotting over home plate.

"I thought I'd do a Texas-style omelet later, lots of stuffing in it. Some toast, too. I haven't had time to do the grocery shopping yet." Tanner frowned at Gwyneth, and noted how he'd really like to put his hands on her round bottom. Under the Rules of Bride Courting, it was her option to ask him to events. With every hour that passed since he'd left Gwyneth's for the Boat Shop— more to keep his hands off her, than to work—he'd waited for her to call. Just as anxious to be away, she'd soared away to parts unknown with a load of new pots and mugs. She'd avoided him until her van cruised up to the shop. "Get in. There's a game tonight," she'd said briskly, eyeing the basic wooden form upon which he'd build a dory.

"Does this mean you're asking me?" he'd specified carefully and straightened, tossing his tool aside.

"I'm in a fix, if I don't show up with you in tow. The whole valley knows about us," she'd muttered darkly.

"Ah. You're in a spot, and now you want to drag me out like a show animal. You haven't had time for me all day and now you want me. How nice. Have you eaten?" he'd asked, noting the setting sun.

She'd blinked at him, a woman unprepared for sharing her life. *Things will have to change, darling,* he'd thought, planning to take very good care of her.

"You didn't come home," she'd accused in a sulky way that eased his bruised pride.

At least she'd missed him in her busy life of taking telephone orders and running the tractor and checking her cattle, he brooded. "I like to be asked, invited you might say, made welcome. A kind word wouldn't hurt. There's telephone lines between your house and the shop. That's what this whole blasted thing is about, isn't it? You making choices? Women asking for dates?''

She'd jammed her fists onto her waist, glaring at him. ''That really burns you, doesn't it? Maybe this small town isn't for you. Maybe you can't fit into the heritage of Freedom Valley. Maybe you want things all your own way. Take a note, Tanner. I'm different. I've changed. I'm not your mother or your sisters, to be pushed around and told what to do. I am your *ex*-wife. I'm not being pushed around anymore, by anyone. And by the way, I didn't like it so much back then, either.''

''Ask,'' he'd demanded, temper and pride ruling him, the image of a bully sitting poorly on his pride.

She'd glared at him. ''I'm asking. Get in.''

At the game, Tanner noted the high fly that Mary Lou Gerard popped into Lacy McDaniel's waiting glove. Lacy threw the softball in a fast, wind-around underhand to Gwyneth at first base. Was this how she felt, sitting on the sidelines, waiting for a look, a glance, a smile while he competed in sports?

''Maybe we could cheerlead for them,'' York noted as fielder Karolina Jones missed an easy catch.

Tanner swilled the icy cola and settled down with his thoughts as Gwyneth neatly caught the next softball the pitcher had lobbed to her, putting another runner out at first base. He didn't like waiting for a call, for her to ask him to come to the game, but finally she had and his heart went merrily flip-flopping away, forgetting all his dark brooding.

''Women,'' he muttered, thinking of how his sisters had each called, wanting details of his progress with Gwyneth, and yelling at him to dust his mother's house. Kylie and Miranda could look feminine and sweet, but to a brother, they were savages when aroused, fearless

as pit bulls, wading into his private life and telling him
what he should do.

"You hurt Gwyneth, and you'll pay," they'd both
promised with threats of removing his scalp, and telling
his future children all the evil he'd done to them.

"You've got to make yourself more appealing, my
man," Fletch was saying.

"I'm plenty appealing. Look who's talking." The
teams changed on the field, batters hit and ran and were
called out, and then Gwyneth was the last batter up, the
score tied. Tanner crushed the empty cola can, lobbed it
into the trash barrel behind him and concentrated on his
woman. She swung, connected with the first pitch and
the softball soared out into field. Rounding the bases,
Gwyneth slid into home plate and the umpire's call was
"safe." The team jumped and cheered around her, and
Tanner shook his head at the long rough red mark on
her bare thigh.

All in all, things weren't too bad. After the game, he
enjoyed the flash of Gwyneth's jaunty grin as she sauntered toward him. "We won," she said, breathlessly,
standing in front of him.

He dabbed a cold rag across her sweaty face, turned
up to him like a child. She'd be a beautiful mother, a
beautiful wife, all the love stored up inside her, waiting
to come out, free of Leather's harshness. "Good job."

"Hah! Better than good. I hit that ball so hard, it went
to the moon."

"Swaggering, arrogant female, full of yourself." He
crouched to inspect her thigh, the red, dirty scrape needing cleaning. Holding the inside of her thigh, just above
her knee, with one hand, he carefully washed the injury
with his other, dipping the rag in a bucket of water.
While he was bending, he retied her loose shoelaces and

when he looked up, the tenderness in her eyes stopped his breath.

"I should have told you," she whispered as the rest of the crowd passed them by, whooping and congratulating her as they went.

She was sorting through the past, laying it in line with who she was now, he knew. There were bits of her coming out, shattered hidden bits, she'd carefully placed into his care. She'd been hurt and taught to keep to herself, but the woman in Gwyneth reached to be free. He stood slowly as the past and the future curled around them. "We'll make it, honey."

"At times, I'm still angry with your mother, for writing what she did, for letting you know. But I'll get over it. I know she loved me. I never saw her so angry. I'm angry at myself for feeling that way about her, that she'd betrayed me. I loved her, too."

"She warned me to give you time. I didn't read the signs, thinking you were young and scared and that we'd have time to—"

She studied his face, searching through all the years. "You wanted to rescue me from Leather, and I wanted to escape. Was it love? Or something else? Would we have made it?"

"We would have," he said firmly as the field lights closed down and the night crickets chirped around them, the cars pulling away from the field. Fredricka, in top shape, was jogging home to her tulip farm, ignoring the whistles from the men passing by. "You're the only woman I'm wanting, sweetheart," Tanner said, answering the question in her hazel eyes.

"You've traveled the world now. You could get bored. Freedom Valley is my home. I'm not likely to pack up—"

Tanner framed her face with his hands. "I've gone over it in my mind. It doesn't matter where we are. We'd have been strong together. Leather was tough, but he would have gone down with the first grandchild—a girl, maybe, who looked like you, with sisters coming soon."

"I thought of that, too. But we're here and now and taking strips off each other. I'm defensive, but you are, too. All the edges leap up with just a word."

"It's all part of knowing each other. Looking back, I don't think we did know each other. You made my head spin, just looking at those dimples. I wasn't thinking clearly. To be truthful, I couldn't wait to take a nibble of that sweet-scented skin."

She smiled softly, delighting him, and then eyed him in a way that caused him to melt. "I'm all sweaty," she said, tossing him her glove and plucking her T-shirt away from her body. "Hot and sweaty."

Would he ever know her moods, quick to be a girl one moment and a woman the next?

"Maybe you need a dip in the lake," he offered, feeling a bit better when her hand slid into his as they walked toward his pickup. "We'll grab a bite at the drive-in, and there will be enough time for it to work off by the time we reach the lake."

"I can't swim and you know it. I used to sit on the bank and watch you show off, swinging from ropes like Tarzan to cannonball into the lake."

"Maybe it's time you learned. You can trust me." The small things, he reminded himself, go for the small things and build from there.

Later, with her bare, wet breasts perfect and sweet in his hands, her wet clinging panties a skimpy barrier to loving her completely, he had to ask, "Do you trust me?"

"Yes," she'd purred, heat pouring from her despite the cool water. "Yes, but hurry...kiss me."

He took his time showing her that he was not a man to hurry and slight the task before him. A thorough and tender craftsman, he pleasured her and kissed her, and told himself to wait for her—because this time Gwyneth would decide.

Nine

Hard times come and they go. But there are sweet times, too, and the knowing that love is right and will endure.

—Anna Bennett

"You're bigger, stronger and tougher," Gwyneth muttered the next day as Tanner shouldered her gently aside. In the late July heat, she was sweaty and frustrated. A half hour in midday temperatures of fighting and coaxing the two new calves, frightened in the trailer behind her van, had torn apart her good mood. Terrified, one had its head stuck between the wooden bars and the other was so frightened, it was leaping and kicking between her and the stuck calf. The red-and-white Hereford calves had been adorable and needing bottle nursing, and they'd stolen her heart. She bartered a new set of bowls for the rancher's wife, and he'd loaded them into the trailer.

Tanner hadn't made love to her, but she'd been well kissed and caressed and awoke with a dreamy smile. Now, the heat and the calves sank her good mood into the field's cow piles.

"You're not so sweet, either. Not right now anyway. I've watched this rodeo too long. Is this what you had to do for Leather? Work like a man?" Tanner demanded crisply, easily corraling the kicking calf and lifting it in his arms. He eased it to the ground and watched it scamper away into the field. "I don't want you hurt."

"There's nothing wrong with hard work—"

"There is when you're overmatched and July's temperature is in the hundreds." He looked nothing like the man who carried breakfast into her room on a tray and had lain down beside her, his hands behind his head. He'd told her some seafaring tale, but she was distracted by his boxer shorts and equipment other than a ship's. The way he took in her T-shirt and the flow of her body beneath the sheet had started her humming; then he took away the breakfast tray and replaced it with himself.

Gwyenth looked at Tanner, managing her task easily in the sweltering heat. She'd lived with a man who mocked her weakness and her gender. "You're taking over my life. Why can't you leave me alone?" she heard herself yell, furious with him as he easily freed the imprisoned calf's head. She detested her harshness, the mark Leather had placed on her—defensive, independent—and so she was unable to give Tanner the woman he needed…though he seemed pretty happy last night when he kissed her at her bedroom door.

Bringing her home without ultimate lovemaking was really what nagged her, but she couldn't let him know it. She didn't know how to give him softness and flirty little smiles. She didn't know what to do with a man who brought in a breakfast tray.

"Why?" His eyes had narrowed as though she'd slapped him. "This is why," he said, reaching to cup the back of her head and fuse his mouth to hers. He'd kissed her roughly, took her heart and her breath and left her standing alone and shaking as he walked, stiff-backed, away from her.

Still gripping her arms around herself, she turned away to view the summer field, dancing with purple clover blooms and swaying white Queen Anne's Lace. She let the teardrops fall then, because she knew she'd hurt him when her moods ran wild, and old Leather's harshness made her lash out at Tanner. She loved him, of course. It was just the showing of it that was hard to do. Could she make him happy? Could she give him—?

The dream that she might please him was too dear, too fragile and she could tear it apart too easily.

She stiffened when Tanner's hands eased to her shoulders and he gathered her back against him, where she was safe and not alone. "Don't worry so, honey. We're coming along fine," he whispered against her cheek. "Mending takes time."

"What can I give you? You've been everywhere. You can charm any woman and probably marry anyone you want. I have nothing to give you—"

He gathered her gently closer to him. "You have yourself and the sweetness of you. You fascinate me, make me laugh, and when I look at you, I get a little woozy, like I'm looking into the future and everything is going to be fine sailing. I even like when we argue, the way your dimples come out when you're in a snit and—oh, when you smile, I think of our little girls and how hard it will be to hold my own against them.''

He paused and inhaled the summer drifting around them, the bumblebees hovering over the clover. ''You give me peace. That's no small thing to give a man.''

Nibbling tantalizingly on the side of her throat, Tanner added, ''Don't think too hard, darling. We're coming along just fine,'' he repeated.

He'd taken away her breath. She lingered in the sweetness and then thought she should repay him in kind.

''You're not so bad, either,'' she whispered, her lips lingering on his rogue's grin.

With a chuckle and caress and a pat on her backside, Tanner left her alone to her thoughts. They were filled with him and that she was a woman with a man to please. *A woman,* she thought, turning the word. Along her life's way, she'd been stripped down, pared into nothing but work, worry and bills. She'd have to think on that, how to be a woman, how to be feminine and enjoy herself. Because Tanner deserved nothing less than a whole woman, who knew what and who she was. ''I'm not trapped anymore,'' she said to the slight breeze carrying the scent of Anna's flower-decked yard to her. ''Anna,'' she whispered, clinging to the memories drifting along in the scents. ''Anna…''

Two weeks later, Freedom Valley was locked in August's hot days and cooler nights. Ella, the sheriff, had let it be known that she didn't want trouble. She was too busy canning tomatoes, making salsa and freezing grated zucchini squash for winter bread and cakes. Fredricka had purchased a huge outdoor trampoline and didn't seem to mind the male audience who slowed their cars during her gymnastics.

Kylie and Miranda had called Gwyneth, and each one's life wasn't going smoothly. They had expected their big brother to dismantle Anna's house, and he couldn't bear to think of it. In quick fashion, Tanner told them to do it themselves, that he wasn't shipping Anna's things to them, but he'd help—if they came home.

She turned her attention back to the big, masculine snag in her life: She'd somehow pictured herself living alone, like the crusty old goat-lady, Billy Jean—and here she was all steamy and living with a man. Tanner was a show-off at times, of course, swaggering around looking all hot and important, and snagging her for a quick kiss when she wasn't expecting it. Because he seemed so excited, grouting and tugging out old rusty pipe and putting in new, she tried not to worry about the cost or what she would owe him.

But at times the worry seized her, and when it did, she took her troubles straight to the troublemaker. Between muscling in the new supersize hot water heater and tearing out walls to enlarge the bathroom with the hallway's space and shifting the front door to the back, Tanner picked up Gwyneth under the arms. He held her easily aloft and scowled at her. "Yes, I know. I'm the bane of your life. I'm in your way, you don't want to be responsible for all the bills I'm running up and all the men around here are wrecking what little peace you have. It's only been two weeks, Gwyneth, and we've redone the kitchen, the windows and—"

Then he kissed her hard and desperately, his look at her steaming. "I want to make love to you every night, in a bed. I want to marry you, and you're taking your time about asking. And hell, no, I'm not calling Kylie and Miranda and making up with them. They can come home, if they want Mom's place settled—and those weren't herbs I pulled from her garden, they were dandelions—''

"Herbs, not dandelions," she argued, noting his hot, frustrated look, the sweat-damp bandanna tied around his forehead. She liked that look, the sulking boy within the man, and sometimes she pricked him just to see his expression.

"I need a laundry room," he muttered, glaring at her, drawing up an ongoing battle about the necessary additions to the house. The disgruntled male holding her up from the floor charged on, deepening his point. "A man has to have a laundry room where he can stand and iron in his shorts."

Gwyneth pressed her lips together, because she wasn't arguing with him now. Arguing with Tanner wasn't like the cut-slice-jab of her father. They were sorting out rules, and Tanner's too-proper kisses at her bedroom door were tearing her. Away from the house, she could nab him until they were both shaking with desire. But once inside the house, Tanner seemed to leash himself, careful of her.

Now she had a mission. To dazzle him. To snag him into her bed. But the doing of that was difficult, because Tanner was either at the shop or working hard with a team of hungry, sweaty commando-type men running up and down ladders and tromping across her roof, and hammering and yelling... She took a deep breath, because now she had Tanner's full attention.

Because her feet were off the ground, one of her shoes plopped to the floor. His dark mood broken, Tanner slowly looked down the length of her body. He blinked and eased her to the floor. "That's a dress," he stated clearly, as though defining a strange animal and labeling it, getting used to the words.

"You miss your sisters. Say it," she prodded, because she didn't dare think of the obvious appreciation in his eyes, the way they lingered at her modest scoop neckline and caressed her breasts.

"Okay. I miss them." The words came softly as he took in her short, light cotton dress, a plain cut with a saucy, midthigh-length hem. Washable and feminine, the catalog dress was on sale and the obvious effect on Tanner made Gwyneth feel very feminine.

Nervous of his reaction, the darkening of his eyes, she scooted her foot into the dropped high-heeled shoe and straightened, smoothing the dress. "It doesn't take a slip," she said, defensive of her purchase. Leather didn't want her having useless "female garb." "How about going to Willa's, just you and me?" she specified because the Bachelor Club was quick to dig into any food nearby. "Then we can go to a drive-in movie."

"It is too hot to shingle anyway," he said, his hands remaining under her arms, but his thumbs cruising over the curves of her breasts. "Are you wanting me, Gwyneth? Are you courting me? Are you going to ask me to marry you?" he added, looking arrogant and rakish, with that wicked, teasing gleam in his eyes.

While she was reeling with his hungry, wolfish look and the hands sliding upward to cover her breasts, a male voice called from the roof, "Hey, Tanner. Here comes the lumber truck. Are we going to put new siding on the house now, or after the new addition is built?"

"New addition?" she asked carefully as Tanner's hands lifted off her breasts and he hooked his thumbs in his jeans, his wary look telling her more than she wanted to know.

"Oh, no. You're not running from this. You just asked

me for a date. Are you taking it back or not?'' he asked
flatly, challenging her.

''Maybe some other time,'' she said when she could
talk. She threw up her hands and reached for the front
door to leave him, to find a quiet little patch of sanity
away from the men churning through her house. The
door wasn't there, because of course, it had been moved
to the back. She glared up at him, and suddenly Tanner
tugged her into his arms, his mouth fierce and possessive
and shielding little of his need from her. Needing him,
too, she grabbed his hair, fisted it, and held his lips to
hers as they kissed, his body already hard and eager for
hers. He eased them into the tiny closet, and ran his
hands over her as though he desperately needed the feel
of her to keep him going. She reveled in that—his need
of her, making his hands tremble and his cheeks flushed
warm against her skin.

''Do you know how hard it is to wait for you?'' he
asked roughly, kissing her again, this time more gently,
tormenting her.

''Everything is changing so,'' she whispered back
against his lips. ''I'm needing you.''

His lips cruised down the sensitive cord at her throat,
taking her heart's tempo faster. ''I'm here to stay, honey.
We're just working out the details between us. I like the
dress,'' he said as his hands slid beneath the hem and
raised it higher. His palms burned her bare hips before
he leaned back, bumping his head on the shelf. While
she rubbed the injury, he looked closely at her. ''You're
trying to seduce me, aren't you?''

Helpless and caught in her plan, she rested against
him. ''I'm feeling very—rosy,'' she said, unable to tell
him how much she loved being with him, to be held by

him. Words came hard to a woman raised by Leather, but they were in her heart.

"We'll have to do something about that, and not like that first time, either," he said darkly, reminding her of how disgusted he'd been with himself that first time. "You can trust me, Gwyneth. I'm here to stay."

"What's that about an addition?"

"It's for a fine big family room and a fine big bedroom, with a fine big bed," he said so firmly that for a moment, she pictured them—

The knock on the closet door and Fidelity's high-pitched wavering voice caused Tanner to groan. He smoothed Gwyneth's hair and her dress and closed his eyes, accepting his fate to be interviewed again by the Women's Council. He looked so resigned and wary that Gwyneth couldn't stop her impulse—she leaned close to his bare chest and suckled his nipple as he had done to her. When she straightened away, stunned by herself, she found Tanner's harsh, tense expression. "Now that was a surprise, Mrs. Bennett," he said roughly.

"Do you like it?" she asked, fearing that her pouncing technique wasn't his favorite. A warm glow began in her and grew into a heady, powerful, wonderful feeling because she knew from his look that he did.

"You sure pick your time," he said darkly. His eyes narrowed and his nostrils flared, and she knew she'd done okay, for her first foray into vamping. "I've got a problem, thanks to you. Stand in front of me when we go out the door," he whispered, reaching past her to open the door to a beaming Fidelity Moore.

"Well, well, well," Fidelity crooned. "Looks like you've passed this inspection, too, Tanner. The dress looks nice on you, Gwyneth, and you're looking quite happy. I see Tanner is making his nest, settling in for the duration. He's a good example to the bachelor boys outside. You've passed inspection once again, Tanner.''

"Thank you, Mrs. Moore,'' he purred, and charmed her more with his smile.

"Boys and toys. So this is why you were gone those two days,'' Gwyneth murmured inside Tanner's houseboat, moored in a cove on Valentina Lake. With just a week until September, the evenings were cool now on the cusp of autumn when the aspens would turn fiery. At sunset, Gwyneth had ridden behind Tanner on a borrowed horse. She'd relaxed, enjoying the long, feminine skirt flirting around her ankles and the man in her arms. The houseboat was like Tanner: practical, neat and with an aura that no woman could resist. She took the glass of wine he handed her and leaned against him. Sunset danced across the water, enclosing them in the sound of lake water lapping against the houseboat, and night settling around the lake. "This feels good.''

Tanner's large hand eased from her waist to her hip and she knew that the time had come for loving, if she wished.

She wished, for his need was there, in his touch and in his eyes. She'd loved a younger Tanner long ago, and she loved him now. "Yes,'' she whispered, letting go of her heart and her fears.

He trembled, and caught by the dying sun on the water, passion glinted in his eyes and honed his face. "This time it will be different,'' he murmured, taking her face in his hands. The kiss was sweet and hungry, making promises for the loving that would come. Then she was in his arms, held tight as he kissed her and carried her inside the houseboat, to the shadows where he would

claim her. When the large bunk was unfolded and neatly
made by Tanner, he turned to her and slowly removed
his clothes. The shadows played along the hard lines of
his body, broad shoulders narrowing to his waist and
gleaming on his hips, his thighs and legs. He came to
her slowly, as if fearing she would run, and the sight of
him was so beautiful, she could not breathe, her heart
filling her chest, beating a wild tattoo there. He gently
unbuttoned her dress and eased the rest away until she
stood in front of him. His hands skimmed over her
shoulders, her arms and lingered, wrapped around her
hands, then slowly his touch came to rest on her breasts
and the shadows danced with his rough, uneven breath.
While looking deep into her eyes as if to catch the first
fear, he placed his hands on her waist, thumbs cruising
over the jut of her hipbones, before wandering to her
backside, filling his palms with her, easing her closer to
him.

With her arms tight around him, Gwyneth moved to
his direction, and then she was on the large bed and
looking up at the man she loved. Again, his gaze stroked
her body, taking in the tangle of feminine and harder
angles, the sweet, soft nestle of her against his jutting
desire. He smoothed her trembling thighs, caressing her
as they became one. With the water lapping against the
boat, the gentle rise and fall of her hips against his,
Gwyneth absorbed all he could give and held him tight.
The lock of their bodies gave her pleasure and then the
lock was tighter, aching, still controlled by Tanner. They
rocked gently as he rose above her, his expression taut
and revealing the strain upon him to move slowly, carefully. The rhythm came faster and she gave herself to
the fireburst running through her body. She fed on his
desperation now, needing him, needing release, and then

Tanner came to her, all of him, with a harsh deep cry, as if it had been torn from his essence.

She held him then in the sweet dark night with the water rocking them and knew that he'd wanted to show her the beauty of making love, the slow sensuality of a man and a woman coming to the ultimate pleasure. He lay beside her, the sheet over them now and the rhythm of his heart, beneath her cheek, slowed and then she slept deeply and safely. She sensed how carefully Tanner treated her, to let her know and feel the gentleness that lovemaking should be. Each time she came more easily to his call, those beautiful strong hands moving over her, tending her as she opened her heart and gave him the same, each kiss taking them deeper.

That dreamy tenderness would wrap around her for days, though Tanner still slept in his bed apart from her. She knew he had his pride and she knew that he waited for her to come to him, to show him that she loved him.

But saying love words and acting like a woman who wanted to entice a man into her bed came hard to the daughter of Leather Smith. "We're doing just fine," Tanner would tell her gently as the days passed.

The big, fine new bed that Tanner had built and placed in the new addition didn't help her concentration and she'd ruined a mug or two. The bed stood boldly on the bare planks of the room, covered in plastic, and surrounded by unfinished walls. It mocked the marriage she had thrown away. She'd loved him then, and she loved him now. But was that enough? Or would the past tear them apart?

Ten

The woman who loves will see through all else,
the good and the bad, and she will have her last
dance, as is the custom of Freedom Valley. It's
not such a bad thing, or an easy thing, either, a
woman making up her mind to claim a man as
her husband and him agreeing to take his time
and tend her carefully. And they will always love,
sharing the last dance. That is what I would have
for my children, as I have had in my life.

—Anna Bennett

The last week of August, Tanner worked in the new
bedroom, finishing the Sheetrock inner walls. It was a
sweet time—a cooling summer rain in the evening, with
Gwyneth working in her studio, their lovemaking in the
barn relaxing his body. She'd caught him there, fixing a

stall that the bull had kicked apart. She'd taken one look, curious hazel eyes tracing the shape of his body, and he'd straightened, tossing away his hammer. She stood still, there in the afternoon sunlight, the scents of hay and animals curling around them. He could have laughed with joy, for her expression said she wanted him, and on her terms.

He'd put the other annoying problem aside, that of a woman he'd long ago known, calling him, wanting him again—the message machine at the Boat Shop left no doubt that Ivana Gordon was prowling. He'd given himself to the look of sheer hunger on Gwyneth's face, the licking of her lips and the dimples he adored. She'd sauntered to him, strolled a finger down his bare chest and looked up at him, learning to toy and please them both. She'd slowly unbuttoned her blouse to show him that she wore nothing, and then she'd eased her breasts against him, watching him beneath her lashes. It had been so sweet, her arms slipping around him until they'd tumbled into the hay. He'd gently taught her how to ride above him, and delighted in the way she curled into herself, hoarding the pleasure that came to them both.

Time, he thought confidently now, finishing the seam between the panels of Sheetrock. *We've got plenty of time.*

Intent on his work, he didn't notice the woman who came to lay her hand on his shoulder. He recognized the expensive scent before he pushed away her hand and turned to look at the woman who had come wanting him. ''That was years ago,'' he said, meaning it, a man bent on a future with a wife he wanted to recapture. ''It's not happening again.''

A man at home and pleased with himself after a shower with the woman he loved, Tanner hadn't both-

ered to snap his jeans. Ivana's hand slid toward the opening, as she stood on tiptoe to push her lush red lips
against his mouth. He captured her hand, holding it away
from him, just as he heard Gwyneth's sharp intake of
breath.

She stood at the unfinished doorway, cuddling a huge
lamp on her hip, the way he'd pictured her holding his
babies one day. Above his borrowed shirt, Gwyneth's
face was pale, patterned by the rain rivulets on the window; her eyes glittered, her mouth tightening. Still she
held the earthenware lamp, her fingers tense on it. *Would
she think that he'd done all this, come to her, loved her,
just for revenge?*

"Gwyneth—" *Was it all gone? The healing swept
away as if it didn't exist? The future killed so easily?*
Tanner thought, panic scurrying through him. All that
they had shared and healed together, lost? "Gwyneth,
this isn't what you think."

Ivana's husky laughter mocked him. "So this is the
little…farmgirl who's been occupying your time. Darling, come back into civilization."

"It was years ago, and it was only one bad night,"
Tanner said slowly, willing himself to speak, to try to
make Gwyneth understand. Trust didn't come easily to
her, but she had been gentling, taking his hand to hold
in a sweet way as she leaned against him. They could
talk now, of Anna and of Leather, and she'd been glad
of his patience and tender lovemaking. He felt that intimacy slip away, replaced by an icy dread of losing
Gwyneth again.

"He might have told you about me. I'm Ivana. We
had a thing, my father owned the shipping line and
would have been quite happy to have Tanner as his son-

in-law," Ivana added, nestling her head on his shoulder and not helping his case with Gwyneth.

Tanner felt the blood run from him, for Gwyneth hadn't moved. She stood in the unfinished doorway, her fingers flexing on the lamp. While the rain quietly tapped on the new windowpanes, a gray evening mist curling around the house, her eyes drifted from Tanner to Ivana and back again, as though she were seeing the relationship, finding the truth of it. He shrugged his shoulder hard enough to dislodge Ivana's head and stood apart from her.

"It didn't matter, and it was years ago," he heard himself repeating, his tone uneven. Afraid Gwyneth wouldn't have him now, Tanner's heart stopped beating, his hands curled into fists. He jerked away from Ivana's hand, from all that was in the past and willed Gwyneth to believe.

"You know," Gwyneth began lightly as she began to walk toward Tanner and Ivana. She moved between them, and shot a sturdy elbow back into his stomach, making him grunt and take a step back. "This is the very first lamp I've made," Gwyneth said too softly to Ivana, and hope began to stir in Tanner. When Gwyneth yelled, her emotions were running free, but when she spoke quietly there was danger on the prowl. Tanner rubbed the slight injury to his stomach and decided to let Gwyneth make her choices. He prayed she would choose him and the truth. He knew from the straight set of her shoulders that Gwyneth had a task before her, and she would do it.

She continued to speak quietly. "This lamp doesn't have its fixtures yet, but I'm proud of it—my first success that didn't fold and crumple and die in the kiln. I have plans to place it beside that fine bed he's made, after we're married again. But I'll gladly smash it over your head if you touch my husband again.''

"Say that again," Tanner ordered harshly after Ivana had fled the room, her sports car tearing away for safety.

Cradling the lamp on her hip with one arm and wildly gesturing with the other, Gwyneth stalked back and forth across the bare planking, her silhouette crossing in front of the windows, gray with rain. He leaned back into the shadows, and crossed his arms over his bare chest. He braced a shoulder against the new walls, a room he hoped to share with Gwyneth, when she made her choice to claim him. She was muttering darkly now, a witch prowling and ready to strike—her eyes slashed at him, branding him as guilty.

"I had other plans—the candle and wine stuff, the soft music, etcetera," she began, while he admired the flitting of his shirt over her curved bottom, and the long, smooth legs gliding back and forth across the room. The dim light from outside was just enough to outline the curve of her breasts—

His hopes inched higher as she glared at him and shot hard words at him across the room. "I shouldn't have you, of course. She knew where to find you. You probably knew she was coming—I won't have you keeping other secrets, Tanner, and I will not have you wearing another woman's lipstick. I'll buy some from Tillie and mark you myself, if I have to. I've asked you for dates. You've passed inspection and came out Grade A. Will you marry me?"

He reached for a rag to wipe away Ivana's lipstick, then crossed his arms again, because he wasn't reaching for Gwyneth too soon this time—she would have to come to him. "Are you asking because of Freedom Valley's customs and how it will look if we don't? Is it your pride that is asking me? Or your anger? Or because I'm the best catch a woman could want? Because I'm smart and charming and handsome and—''

''You're full of yourself, Mr. Bennett,'' she murmured with a slow, enchanting smile that set his heart racing. ''You were caught, though, for a moment, scowling and ready to snarl, if I didn't believe you.''

''Come here, Mrs. Bennett.'' He couldn't wait for her, his body needing hers, the woman of his heart. He enjoyed that stubborn, weighing look, because his love was making her choices, placing aside the precious lamp and straightening. His old blue chambray shirt, soft and worn and spotted with glazes and clay, drifted around her body as she strolled to him.

He kept his arms crossed over his chest, pressing the wild beat of his heart. He would have his due, for his pride and because he needed to have the words. ''Say it,'' he ordered, as she placed her hands along his jaw, stroking the evening stubble.

Shadows played along her lashes, but her eyes locked with his, the time for truth had come. ''I've always loved you. I knew back then that you would be the man you are today—kind, loving, perfect—just what Anna said you would be. But I didn't know me. I had to learn to stand on my own. To know that I was strong and could face the past. You've shown me that—that Leather gave me hardships, but he gave me strength, too. Those men took something I know you valued, and I needed time to heal. I was trapped, though, unable to move on. Then you came back—swaggering, foul-tempered, beast of a man, meddling in my life,'' she added with a kiss on his chin.

''We'll have the last dance then, at the Women's Council Fall Dance,'' he said unsteadily, needing the confirmation. He feared that he was dreaming as he looked into her eyes and the future he'd dreamed of long ago. "You'll marry me."

"Pushy, old-fashioned man. Needing to state ideas like they were yours and not mine," she teased. But she nodded, her steady look a promise. "And I really wish you wouldn't hold back when we make love. You won't hurt me and I won't break and I'm expecting the truth of what you feel, not only with words, with your body. Because you love me. You always have, and I have always been married to you, no matter what words were written on paper."

Then he could wait no more, dragging her to him for the kiss he needed desperately to take, to hold her close and safe and know that all the years weren't gone or wasted—they were just beginning.

They made love softly on the new bed with the rain making patterns on the windows and on their intertwined bodies. The first time was the pledge of their lives, the second was the hunger he could no longer shield from her, his claiming, a primitive need to take his wife, the other half of his heart, with the emotions ruling him. He tore away the sheet that he'd drawn over them as they rested from the first time and the sight of her soft body tangled with his darker one set him off, for the bond was forged deep now and all pretenses were torn away, but the one—his driving need to find her in the ultimate shocking heat, to free himself of leashes and love her without restraint. *Did he dare? Would the fierce heart of him frighten her? Would he tear apart what they had built?*

"Yes," she whispered as he placed his hand on her breasts, noting the harshness that was within him and the softness he treasured. Torn between his desire and his fear that he would shock her, Tanner trembled, skimming his hand over her body, down to the darkness where he hoped to place his child—if Gwyneth chose the dream for her own.

She rose to gently nip his shoulder and the slight injury tore away the shield to his hunger. He gave her a moment, her face pale in the night, to see him coming, to know that he would release to her that stark, driving hunger, his passionate desire for her, the woman he loved.

He bent to taste her breast, to suckle in the way that brought her hips surging against him, her nails digging into his shoulder. She pushed him away slightly, then brought him back, a woman who would have her due and meet him evenly this time, their hearts one, as their bodies would be. He took her wrist, needing the shackling image to know that he would keep her all their lives. She tugged it slightly away, just to let him know he couldn't have all things his way. They looked at each other and found the truth. He moved his thigh over her and she moved away, resisting, then letting herself be captured. He placed his body over hers, the moist calling of her body enticing his. He surged into her, inhaling as she took him tightly. Holding her wrists on the pillow, he sunk deep to claim her and then Gwyneth's legs lifted higher, capturing him in her own way. He tested her strength, drawing slightly away and she drew him back, letting him know that she would come after him, should he have any other notions. He tested the fit again, lifting away, and then sinking deeper as Gwyneth's thighs enclosed his hips tightly. She rose to take his mouth, to nip gently on his bottom lip and then fall back, watching him, a woman set to entice and take and give.

Her hips threw him back and met and took and soon, the wild singing in his blood shot to a feverish heat, her arms wrapping around him as his hands went beneath her. The fast pace of hungry kisses, feasting and teasing and burning brought the swift pulse to them both, passion surging higher, blinding him with the beat—

"Oh, no," she sighed, pushing him away and moving over him, and then the tempo began again. Instantly she stilled, his mouth on her breasts, capturing, nibbling and dragging to the other. She braced her hands on his chest, fingers digging in as that first ripple coursed through her. Because he would have his due this time, Tanner turned her again, lost in his need for her. Her gripping body took his and with a shout, he gave himself to her.

"I love it when you look like that, all hot and fierce and masterful, as if nothing can stop you from having me…like nothing could ever tear you from me—ever. The sweet, tender look isn't too bad, either. Thank you for waiting, for understanding, for trying," she whispered as his head rested on her breasts and her leg leisurely rose up and down, caressing his. He managed to turn his head to kiss her tenderly, but the rest of his body floated happily beside his love. Later, he would tell her more, the fullness that was in him, the peace he'd found. He held her in his arms all night, awakening to find her snuggled close to him.

She nestled her head on his shoulder, as if testing it for a lifetime, draped her soft thigh over his, her arm around him, and whispered. "Gotcha."

Tanner grinned against her hair. "Okay."

He'd danced with Fidelity, Mary Lou and all the ladies of the Council and now he waited impatiently for his love, the wife he'd always held in his heart. They'd

be remarried soon, amid September's fiery color, and
sooner if he had his way, but this time, Gwyneth would
have to do the arranging, not Anna. Kylie and Miranda
would be in the middle of the fiesta, as would the ladies
of Freedom Valley. This time, Gwyneth could hold her
own with his wildfire, hot-tempered sisters. Tanner's
friends, The Bachelor Club, would be holing up, working on their boats and grumbling about the hoopla.
They'd act silly when the babies came along, and Gwyneth was anxious to start on the new project as soon as
possible. The first girl they'd name Anna.

When the band leader called "Last Dance," Tanner
found his love coming for him. The jade-green dress had
been carefully sewn, in the hours Gwyneth used Anna's
old machine. She hid away in his mother's house
wrapped in memories, making her peace with the past
and planning her future. She'd be careful with Anna's
tea towels and pillowcases and tablecloths nestling in her
hope chest at the foot of their bed. She'd bring them out
for special occasions, and for the wedding, she'd wear
lace that Anna had crocheted. Gwyneth tended Anna's
house, but she'd made it known to Kylie and Miranda
that they would have to do their share—because she'd
be too busy raising a herd of Tanner's babies and keeping him safe from "poachers." Her custom-made lamp
business and ranching on a smaller scale would take up
the rest of her time.

Tanner allowed himself a smile, because Kylie and
Miranda were in for a surprise—little Gwyneth was now
a woman, who knew her own mind and wasn't being
pushed.

"This is the last dance. Will you dance with me?"
Gwyneth asked, her hand slipping into his.

"For all my life," he returned, drawing her close, this woman of his heart, of his soul.

While Tanner and Gwyneth danced in their love and their dreams, Fidelity Moore tapped her cane upon the floor. The women of Freedom Valley smiled because they knew that the Rules for Bride Courting had been proven once more. They eyed the Bachelor Club—tall, wary men coveyed in a corner for protection—and wondered who would be next.... "They come from good stock—the Founding Mothers," Fidelity noted, trying to give good points to the proven rakes that they were. "Love can be contagious...Mary Lou, see that more copies of the *Women's Council's Rules for Bride Courting* are at the ready and make plenty of inspection sheets. We're going to need them."

* * * * *

Cait London fans are in for an extra special treat in August 2000—another sensual, emotional TALLCHIEF *love story! Don't dare miss*

TALLCHIEF: THE HOMECOMING,

part of Silhouette Desire's brand-new Body and Soul promotion, featuring extra powerful, passionate and provocative romances!

SILHOUETTE'S 20TH ANNIVERSARY CONTEST
OFFICIAL RULES
NO PURCHASE NECESSARY TO ENTER

1. To enter, follow directions published in the offer to which you are responding. Contest begins 1/1/00 and ends on 8/24/00 (the "Promotion Period"). Method of entry may vary. Mailed entries must be postmarked by 8/24/00, and received by 8/31/00.

2. During the Promotion Period, the Contest may be presented via the Internet. Entry via the Internet may be restricted to residents of certain geographic areas that are disclosed on the Web site. To enter via the Internet, if you are a resident of a geographic area in which Internet entry is permissible, follow the directions displayed on-line, including typing your essay of 100 words or fewer telling us "Where In The World Your Love Will Come Alive." On-line entries must be received by 11:59 p.m. Eastern Standard time on 8/24/00. Limit one e-mail entry per person, household and e-mail address per day, per presentation. If you are a resident of a geographic area in which entry via the Internet is permissible, you may, in lieu of submitting an entry on-line, enter by mail, by hand-printing your name, address, telephone number and contest number/name on an 8"x 11" plain piece of paper and telling us in 100 words or fewer "Where In The World Your Love Will Come Alive," and mailing via first-class mail to: Silhouette 20th Anniversary Contest, (in the U.S.) P.O. Box 9069, Buffalo, NY 14269-9069; (In Canada) P.O. Box 637, Fort Erie, Ontario, Canada L2A 5X3. Limit one 8"x 11" mailed entry per person, household and e-mail address per day. On-line and/or 8"x 11" mailed entries received from persons residing in geographic areas in which Internet entry is not permissible will be disqualified. No liability is assumed for lost, late, incomplete, inaccurate, nondelivered or misdirected mail, or misdirected e-mail, for technical, hardware or software failures of any kind, lost or unavailable network connection, or failed, incomplete, garbled or delayed computer transmission or any human error which may occur in the receipt or processing of the entries in the contest.

3. Essays will be judged by a panel of members of the Silhouette editorial and marketing staff based on the following criteria:

   Sincerity (believability, credibility)—50%

   Originality (freshness, creativity)—30%

   Aptness (appropriateness to contest ideas)—20%

   Purchase or acceptance of a product offer does not improve your chances of winning. In the event of a tie, duplicate prizes will be awarded.

4. All entries become the property of Harlequin Enterprises Ltd., and will not be returned. Winner will be determined no later than 10/31/00 and will be notified by mail. Grand Prize winner will be required to sign and return Affidavit of Eligibility within 15 days of receipt of notification. Noncompliance within the time period may result in disqualification and an alternative winner may be selected. All municipal, provincial, federal, state and local laws and regulations apply. Contest open only to residents of the U.S. and Canada who are 18 years of age or older, and is void wherever prohibited by law. Internet entry is restricted solely to residents of those geographical areas in which Internet entry is permissible. Employees of Torstar Corp., their affiliates, agents and members of their immediate families are not eligible. Taxes on the prizes are the sole responsibility of winners. Entry and acceptance of any prize offered constitutes permission to use winner's name, photograph or other likeness for the purposes of advertising, trade and promotion on behalf of Torstar Corp. without further compensation to the winner, unless prohibited by law. Torstar Corp and D.L. Blair, Inc., their parents, affiliates and subsidiaries, are not responsible for errors in printing or electronic presentation of contest or entries. In the event of printing or other errors which may result in unintended prize values or duplication of prizes, all affected contest materials or entries shall be null and void. If for any reason the Internet portion of the contest is not capable of running as planned, including infection by computer virus, bugs, tampering, unauthorized intervention, fraud, technical failures, or any other causes beyond the control of Torstar Corp. which corrupt or affect the administration, secrecy, fairness, integrity or proper conduct of the contest, Torstar Corp. reserves the right, at its sole discretion, to disqualify any individual who tampers with the entry process and to cancel, terminate, modify or suspend the contest or the Internet portion thereof. In the event of a dispute regarding an on-line entry, the entry will be deemed submitted by the authorized holder of the e-mail account submitted at the time of entry. Authorized account holder is defined as the natural person who is assigned to an e-mail address by an Internet access provider, on-line service provider or other organization that is responsible for arranging e-mail address for the domain associated with the submitted e-mail address.

5. Prizes: Grand Prize—a $10,000 vacation to anywhere in the world. Travelers (at least one must be 18 years of age or older) or parent or guardian if one traveler is a minor, must sign and return a Release of Liability prior to departure. Travel must be completed by December 31, 2001, and is subject to space and accommodations availability. Two hundred (200) Second Prizes—a two-book limited edition autographed collector set from one of the Silhouette Anniversary authors: Nora Roberts, Diana Palmer, Linda Howard or Annette Broadrick (value $10.00 each set). All prizes are valued in U.S. dollars.

6. For a list of winners (available after 10/31/00), send a self-addressed, stamped envelope to: Harlequin Silhouette 20th Anniversary Winners, P.O. Box 4200, Blair, NE 68009-4200.

Contest sponsored by Torstar Corp., P.O. Box 9042, Buffalo, NY 14269-9042.

PS20RULES

ENTER FOR
A CHANCE TO WIN*

Silhouette's 20th Anniversary Contest

Tell Us Where in the World
You Would Like *Your* Love To Come Alive...
And We'll Send the Lucky Winner There!

Silhouette wants to take you wherever
your happy ending can come true.

Here's how to enter: Tell us, in 100 words or less,
where you want to go to make your love come alive!

In addition to the grand prize, there will be 200
runner-up prizes, collector's-edition book sets
autographed by one of the Silhouette anniversary
authors: **Nora Roberts, Diana Palmer,
Linda Howard** or **Annette Broadrick**.

DON'T MISS YOUR CHANCE TO WIN!
ENTER NOW! No Purchase Necessary

Silhouette®
Where love comes alive™

Visit Silhouette at www.eHarlequin.com to enter, starting this summer.

Name:

Address:

City: State/Province:

Zip/Postal Code:

Mail to Harlequin Books: **In the U.S.**: P.O. Box 9069, Buffalo, NY
14269-9069; **In Canada**: P.O. Box 637, Fort Erie, Ontario, L4A 5X3

*No purchase necessary—for contest details send a self-addressed stamped envelope to:
Silhouette's 20th Anniversary Contest, P.O. Box 9069, Buffalo, NY, 14269-9069 (include
contest name on self-addressed envelope). Residents of Washington and Vermont may
omit postage. Open to Cdn. (excluding Quebec) and U.S. residents who are 18 or over.
Void where prohibited. Contest ends August 31, 2000.   PS20CON_R2